Man in the Moon

by

K. A. Young

Quitman, Texas is a real place, but all persons in this story are fictitious. No character represents any real individual, alive or deceased. No single church is solely represented. Private homes are entirely imaginary. Public places are or were real.

Second Edition

WDP
Whyte Dove Press
Quitman, Texas

Man in the Moon

by

K. A. Young

Published by:

WDP

Whyte Dove Press
Quitman, TX

Scripture quotations are taken from the Authorized King James Version.

Library of Congress Cataloging-in-Publication Data
Young, K. A.
  Man in the moon / by K. A. Young. – 2nd ed.
  Quitman, Tex.: Whyte Dove Press, 2017. -- 120 p. : ill.
  Summary: An imaginative little girl who stutters wants to win friends by starring in a play and to help solve the mystery of the Holiday Hoodlum.
  [1. Fiction, Juvenile. -- 2. Social interaction in children—Fiction. 3. Stuttering in children—Fiction. -- 4. Christian ethics—Fiction. 5. Small towns—Fiction.]   I. Title.
            ISBN 978-0-9708999-6-5 (pbk.)

This book is lovingly dedicated to
my grandchildren.

Acknowledgements

Many thanks to the following people who helped turn my dream, this book, into a reality—and then improved on it.

My Creator gave me the love of words, imagination, and discipline to complete this book. My loving supportive husband never gave up on me nor let me give up. My grandmothers and grandchildren inspired me to share a bit of myself in this work of fiction, and my son shared his time and talents in support of me.

Karen Blalock edited for content. Her valuable suggestions greatly improved the book. JoAnne Barrett edited for grammar and usage, saving me from embarrassment. Helen Perry checked page layouts, catching visual errors to which I remained blind. They are the reason I haven't found a typo yet.

Members of the Whyte Dove Writers' Group encouraged and guided me in the publication of the first edition in 2001. The members of this group now have encouraged and guided me in the publication of this second edition. Without them, I would not have finished this book or begun the next.

Jordan Smith, Joleen Yeager with Victoria and Nathaniel, Kim Shirley with Randy and Beka, Vicki Clark and others previously mentioned provided reviews. Many family and friends assisted me in this project and prayed for its success.

Cindy Powdrill, a teacher at Gladewater ISD, took my book into her classroom and allowed me a place in her sixth-grade readers' hearts. Newton ISD and Quitman ISD teachers and students supported the book, these sharing their names with the characters: Rose, Raven, Chris, and Steve. Wood County residents make it a fine place to live, to work, and to write about.

This book developed from two assignments in the excellent course I took from the Institute of Children's Literature.

I humbly thank all these and my parents and teachers for teaching me to read and write and for giving me opportunities to do both in abundance.

Table of Contents

Chapter 1   The Drama Class 7

Chapter 2   The Letter 17

Chapter 3   The Vampire 25

Chapter 4   The Witness 31

Chapter 5   The Indian Princess 37

Chapter 6   The Homework 41

Chapter 7   The Leading Role 45

Chapter 8   The Revenge 49

Chapter 9   The Answer 55

Chapter 10   The Understudy 59

Chapter 11   The Play 63

Chapter 12   The Spies 67

Chapter 13   The Theft 71

Chapter 14   The Police 77

Chapter 15   The Plan 81

Chapter 16   The Night Out 87

Chapter 17   The Lost Time 95

Chapter 18   The Discovery 101

Chapter 19   The Spotlight 109

Chapter 20   The Snow Queen 113

Chapter 21   The Birthday 117

Page Intentionally Blank

Chapter 1

The Drama Class

*I*t was that laughter again. A brisk October breeze swept dry leaves and the sound of that laughter down the covered sidewalk as Maxey Dove and the other sixth-graders scurried to their classes. Classrooms opened onto outdoor walkways at Quitman Elementary. Maxey shivered—more from dread than from cold—as she scanned the throng in the direction of the laughter. Attending a small school in a small town, she knew every sixth-grader and most of the younger children, too. She knew that laughter. It was the kind that ridicules, and it had often been aimed at her. Seconds later she spied Bubba and Rusty, shuffling down the sidewalk.

Bubba was a tall round boy with glasses. Rusty was a short stocky one with red hair and freckles. They pushed and shoved anyone in their way. Maxey plastered her slender body to the wall, imagining herself so thin she was invisible.

Just then, she heard a distinct sound in the cacophony: someone humming off-key. It was her once-upon-a-time best friend, Angel McGregor. Angel was striding her way in a neon

blue wind suit that shimmered against her long, blazing red curls. On her feet were spotless white sneakers.

Maxey observed the powdery red dirt of the playground coloring the edges of the sidewalk opposite the building. Its stain drew menacingly close to Angel's white sneakers. The bullies were speeding toward Angel like an eighteen-wheeler. Maxey knew she must do something.

She peeled herself from the brick wall, her waist-length thin brown hair clinging like cobwebs to the masonry. She jerked her head sideways, pulling her hair back to herself. She dropped her books on the sidewalk.

To be brave, swift, and strong, she knew she must reach beyond herself. She needed to be more than a little girl to face her enemies. She would be Shadow, the black wolf. With all her imagination, she made the transformation. She could feel the change inside herself. She faced the bullies and bared her teeth.

No, Maxey told herself, *they don't see Shadow—only a little girl.* It was so confusing these days to know when to pretend and when to play it safe. *Be careful not to let it show. Let them be surprised that you didn't cringe or back off in fear.*

"Hey, Weirdo, whatcha grinnin' at?" Rusty asked, sneering.

Bubba clasped Maxey's shoulder with his meaty palm and shoved her backwards right into Angel.

Angel stumbled and fell, rolling off the sidewalk into the red dirt. Her face was nearly as red as her hair, making her blue eyes appear bluer still. They were icy blue—ice daggers that hurt Maxey just to look at them.

Maxey groaned. She thought, *It happened again. Nothing is ever like I imagine. I felt strong and brave, like Shadow, but I wasn't. I was just...me.*

She never knew how to act. If she was herself, she felt ridiculous. If she was different, everyone else thought she was ridiculous. They called her a weirdo—and worse. *I'm not weird—am I?*

Angel stood and brushed herself off. "Maxey Dove, get out of my way. I don't want to be late to drama class." She ran down the sidewalk, disappearing into the room four doors away.

Maxey stooped to pick up her trapper-keeper notebook and paperback novel from the sidewalk. *Yeah, it's the first day of drama class*, she thought. *I don't want to be late either.*

Maxey had taken music and art the first and second six weeks. She had enjoyed both, but drama would be best. In drama class, you were expected to pretend. Since Maxey was good at pretending, she thought she could get the others to like her by doing well in a play. Ever since school began that year, she had imagined getting the leading role. She told herself: *If I do, Daddy will come all the way from wherever-he-is to see me—if he's not filming a movie.*

Skipping along past three classrooms, she stopped before reaching the fourth, stood still, and closed her eyes. In her mind, she could see a stage—curtains drawn back with lights all around, the audience like a pool of inky water with faces floating here and there on the surface. Her father sat in the front row, his face bathed in light. She had trouble remembering what he looked like. Everyone was applauding—even Angel and her other classmates. Maxey's father was clapping loudest of all.

As Maxey imagined all of this, she bowed. She bowed again and again.

When she looked up, she saw Mrs. Cannon standing in the doorway of the classroom, studying her. Mrs. Cannon was the new teacher of sixth grade drama.

Mrs. Cannon smiled down at her and held the door open for her. Mrs. Cannon was tall, large, and dark with thick black hair braided in coils piled high on her head. She reminded Maxey of a picture in her Bible story book of the Queen of Sheba, an African lady of great wealth and stature who once visited King Solomon, the wisest man who ever lived.

"Miss Dove?"

Maxey stammered, "I..I'm s..sorry for being l..late."

Mrs. Cannon said, "Have a seat. We're glad you're here."

Maxey was fascinated by Mrs. Cannon. Her teeth were enormous white rectangles like piano keys. *Like a grand piano.* Her voice was deep and warm. *Like a cello.* Maxey had learned about grand pianos and cellos in music class.

While finding a place to sit, Maxey looked for Angel. Rose Ravenwood had already grabbed the seat next to her. So Maxey sat in the desk directly behind Angel. The back of Angel's red curls billowed like a fire, like the picture of Moses' burning bush Maxey recalled seeing at church the day before.

Maxey tried to convey a message telepathically to Angel: *You're MY friend.* Angel was laughing at something Rose whispered in her ear. *How can you read my mind if you won't pay attention?* Maxey concentrated.

Maxey listened with her mind but got no response. Like seeing the handwriting on the wall, a Bible story Maxey learned in church, she realized her friendship with Angel was doomed if something didn't change. *But what?*

Mrs. Cannon finished taking roll and began to talk about the power of imagination. She told how people had been acting out stories since long before they could write them down. She described the history of theater with sweeping gestures that seemed to extend beyond the panorama of the classroom, flinging Maxey's thoughts clear beyond the universe itself—into the realm of fantasy.

Maxey sat up straight in her chair. Her ears gobbled every syllable as if they had been starved for this revelation. Nobody spoke like Mrs. Cannon. *Could it be...possible...that Mrs. Cannon believes in the man in the moon?* Maxey leaned forward. She didn't want to miss a word.

Mrs. Cannon announced, "We'll be working on two plays during these next six weeks. You can try out for parts in the

Thanksgiving play next week. We'll begin work on the winter play right after the Thanksgiving holidays."

Maxey took a deep breath to keep from shouting. *I'll have the leading role in two plays*! she promised herself.

"This week," Mrs. Cannon continued, "we'll get acquainted with lines from famous plays. As I hand you a selection, say the words to yourself. Hear their rhythm in your head. Think of what they mean, how they make you feel."

Mrs. Cannon handed each child a paper.

Maxey stared at hers. The ink-stained paper was a sea of pale purple, and bluish-purple letters swam in it like exotic fish.

"These are mimeographed copies," Mrs. Cannon explained to the class, "not photocopies. As I call your name, read your selection to the class."

Maxey's head jerked up like a fish being yanked out of water. Her eyes were huge and staring, her mouth open. She gasped as though unable to breathe. *Not me*, thought Maxey. *But then, why give me this paper?* Maxey wiped her clammy hands on her jeans. Her mouth was so dry it felt full of cotton.

None of the teachers in the small northeast Texas town of Quitman had ever made Maxey read out loud. But Mrs. Cannon was new to the community, having taught in Houston the year before. Maxey couldn't be certain Mrs. Cannon wouldn't call on her to read aloud. All she could do was hope that didn't happen.

Trembling, she tried to concentrate on the paper. She mouthed the title: "From Hamlet." Without warning, she imagined a giant ham omelet and a giant hand cutting a piece of it with a giant fork. Nervously, she giggled.

"Maxine," Mrs. Cannon said sharply.

Maxey lowered her head.

Mrs. Cannon stood in front of the row where Maxey sat in the third desk, cowering behind Angel. Mrs. Cannon towered over them. Mrs. Cannon's penetrating gaze drew Maxey's gray-green eyes into an unwilling embrace. *Mrs. Cannon's dark*

12

eyes...so round...warm brown...like my stuffed koala's...like chocolate. Her eyes held Maxey's until Maxey almost smiled.

Mrs. Cannon said softly, "Maxine, you can read first."

Maxey could feel the stares of the other children like flaming darts, making her face hot. She tried to lick her lips, but her tongue was like a wild horse and her lips were as prickly as a cactus.

"T..t..to be," she squeaked, "or n..n..not t..to be. Th..that is th..the question. Wheth..th..ther 't..t..tis n..n..nobler in th..the mind t..t..to s..s..s..suffer...."

Mrs. Cannon interrupted. She said pleasantly, "That's all right for now, Maxine. You stick with it and you'll be rendering Shakespeare eloquently."

A boy in the back of the class asked, "Doesn't render mean rip apart?"

Several of the other kids snickered.

Another boy asked, "Who's Shakespeare?"

Angel declared, "Mrs. Cannon means Maxey can ruin the works of the most famous writer in the English language."

Maxey slid down in her seat until her head pressed against the back of her desk chair. She tried imagining her old pink sweatshirt was a kitten's tongue, lapping her up from this awful place and setting her down to play in a saucer of warm milk. In her mind, Maxey stuck out her tongue at Angel. She stared at Angel's hair, knowing her own face was as red. *Why does Angel hate me?* she wondered, blinking back tears that threatened to scald her already burning cheeks.

Mrs. Cannon was saying, "...not the same meaning as the word 'rend.' Rendering means performing and eloquently means persuasively. Angel is correct as to the identity of Shakespeare, but she entirely missed my meaning. I'm sure Maxine can learn to read Shakespeare as the Bard himself intended."

"Not in this life," said a girl across the room.

Angel giggled.

Maxey glared at her.

Mrs. Cannon clapped her hands twice, and in a voice that commanded more attention than the lunch bell, she said, "That's enough." Her frown silenced the class.

Then, in her cello-like voice, she asked, "Who would like to read next?"

Maxey refused to listen to her classmates read. *I wish their tongues would turn black and fall off. Especially Angel's.*

Trying to ignore Mrs. Cannon, Maxey looked around the room. Colorful posters hung on the walls: a circus, a black horse pawing at the air, a castle with pennants. Book covers hung between the posters. Maxey liked the one with the white wolf on it. Piles of books leaned on shelves along the wall in the back of the room near a table and chairs. Maxey wanted to sit back there, away from everybody else, and lose herself in a storybook.

The drama class had started out all wrong. Angel had nearly ruined it for her. Maxey itched to get even but ached to be friends again. She wished she could pretend to be a talking rabbit with a small pink nose and soft gray whiskers. She'd hop right up to Angel and tell her she wanted them to be friends again. Angel liked rabbits. She wanted Angel to like her again.

No, Maxey told herself, *Angel won't like it if you pretend to be a rabbit. She doesn't like playing make-believe anymore.* Maxey decided to talk it over with Angel even if she had to do it without pretending, even if she had to do it just being herself.

Mrs. Cannon was saying, "...time to go home now. Read your selection to an adult who will sign a note saying you did so. Bring the selections and signed notes to class on Wednesday."

As Maxey stuffed the purple paper in her trapper-keeper notebook, she thought, *I'm not reading this to Mama. She'd die if she knew I was in a drama class.*

The bell rang and everyone raced through the door.

Outside, Maxey shouted, "Angel, wait!"

Angel put her hands on her hips and let Maxey catch up.

Maxey said, "L..let's be friends again. Just s..say you're s..sorry for being mean, and I..I'll forgive you."

Angel shook her head, her red curls bouncing. "I'm not the one who should be sorry. You always act so strange, Maxey. Who wants to be friends with a weirdo?" Angel ran off.

Maxey hung her head. *What's the use? If I pretend to be something else or if I'm just myself, nobody likes me anyway.*

Chapter 2

The Letter

Maxey kicked at the dry pine needles and crisp fallen leaves—oak, sassafras, dogwood, and black gum—all the way home to the Wilson Apartments. The acrid smell of someone's burn pile scratched her nostrils. The harsh reality of her lost friendship with Angel scratched her mind. She snorted.

Maxey and Angel had enjoyed playing make-believe over the summer. When school began, though, Angel avoided her. *I just don't get it.* As Maxey mulled this over in her mind, she spotted Rory playing in the yard between their apartments and waved at him. Rory ignored her as he always seemed to do since he turned thirteen. *I don't get that either. I'm not so much younger than Rory. I'll be eleven in a couple of months.*

Rory was kicking and jabbing the air.

Maxey asked, "Who are you fighting th..this t..time?

Rory scowled, "Nobody."

"Th..that's n..not much fun."

"I'm practicing karate. My friend, Brandon, takes lessons in Mineola. He's been showing me some moves. REAL karate."

"T..teach me."

Rory sneered. "No way! You'd just be making up stuff."

"What's wrong with th..that?"

Rory scowled at Maxey again and replied, "It's all you ever do, Maxey. Get real." He turned around and punched the air, ignoring her.

She kicked dirt at him. The wind twirled it around his feet. Recalling *Wizard of Oz*, a video her mother had rented from Movie Gallery, she imagined a tornado was carrying Rory north—past Winnsboro, far away from Texas to someplace like Kansas. *I wouldn't click my heels to bring you home, Rory.*

She climbed the steps of the front porch to her apartment and went inside.

Her mother sat in the armchair across the room, watching TV. Her feet were propped on the stool Maxey had used years ago to reach the bathroom sink.

Maxey said, "Hi, Mama," as she stumbled through her bedroom door to the right. She dropped her books on her bed and then walked through the living room into the kitchen.

She sniffed. No nice smells wafted from the oven. Nothing on top of the stove or in the sink looked like supper waiting to happen.

Maybe Mama's back was hurting her again. She worked an early shift at the Village Manor Nursing Home, leaving before Maxey went to school and getting home just before Maxey did. Mama liked her job, helping the older people. Sometimes, though, when she had to lift somebody in or out of bed, she strained her back and didn't feel like doing much when she got home. *That must be it*, Maxey told herself.

"Can I..I get a s..snack?" Maxey called to her mother.

No answer.

Since no answer wasn't the same as a "no" answer, Maxey got two miniature banana-flavored moon pies from the cabinet and milk from the refrigerator. She sat at the kitchen table, munching the first one.

Umm. Moon pies are yummy. She licked her lips and kicked the table leg. Lick-kick-lick-kick.

Why doesn't Mama yell at me to stop? Maxey guessed there must be something especially interesting on television.

Oprah maybe.

After gulping the last drop of milk in her glass, Maxey poured some more. SPLAT! It sloshed out, forming a puddle of milk on the floor that looked to Maxey like a.... *Like what? Like an ice rink.* Maxey dropped the last crumbs from her first moon pie onto the pool of milk and pretended they were skaters in yellow jackets and tights, twirling and spinning on an ice-covered pond.

Suddenly the volume on the TV blared. Commercials. *Mama always mutes the commercials*, Maxey recalled. *Or she gets a snack. I'd better get this milk up off the floor!* She sopped up the mess with fistfuls of paper towels while peering into the living room. Mama seemed mesmerized. Oprah was on.

Carefully, Maxey unwrapped her other mini-moon-pie and studied it. It was yellow just like a banana. But round like a full moon. With her pointing finger, Maxey poked two holes in the moon pie for eyes. Then she poked another hole underneath the eyes for a nose. She got a fork from the silverware drawer and made lots of tiny holes across the bottom for a smile. Viewing her artwork triumphantly, she said to herself, *YES! It looks just like the man in the moon.*

Maxey contemplated the face she had made. She thought, *Except for me...and maybe Mrs. Cannon...nobody believes in him anymore.*

Maxey couldn't bring herself to eat the little moon pie with a face. Instead, she wrapped it in a piece of paper towel and took it to her room to hide it from her mother. She stood on the corner of her toy box and leaned into the closet where she tried to put it on the top shelf. It slipped from her fingers. She

slipped off the corner of the toy box. BUMP. *Quick!—before Mama comes!* Maxey scooped the moon pie off the floor, checked to see if it's face still looked okay, which it did, and then tucked it into a corner of the toy box. *Mama's bound to come running in here any second to see what's the matter.*

Instead, Mama just sat in the living room in front of the TV without a word. Maxey thought, *Mama's back never hurt her THIS much. What's going on?* She decided to ask her mother what was for supper and tell her she'd need help with her math homework.

As Maxey approached her, the light of the TV revealed Mama's face and eyelashes were wet. *Uh-oh. Mama's been crying. She really MUST be hurt.*

In Mama's lap was a letter—many pages, all stapled in the corner—curled up in two folds like a roly-poly bug on its back. The flat middle part rested on her blue jeans like a water lily floating on a pond, reminding Maxey of the picture of a famous painting by Claude Monet she had seen in art class. The letter had fancy writing at the top: Rainwater, Nichols, something-or-other, and Luck. It made Maxey think of the tale about finding a pot of gold at the end of the rainbow.

She wondered if her Mama had tried to find it and the leprechaun had written: "Sorry you didn't win this time. Please try again." Maxey was sad, too, whenever she peeled the white paper off the inside of a bottle cap and read "Try Again" instead of "Free Fries" or "You're a Winner!" She didn't cry about it, though. *Maybe Mama was going to win millions.* She reached for the letter to read how much money Mama had tried to win.

Her mother snatched the letter from her and chunked it across the room. Its pages rattled as it flew toward the television. Maxey remembered the white goose she had startled the time she visited the Caldwell Zoo in Tyler. That goose flew right out of the water! Now Maxey believed she knew how the goose had felt. *Mama is startling me.*

Mama snapped, "I wait and wait. What does it get me?"

Maxey couldn't think of anything to say.

"That!" Mama shouted, pointing at the letter, lying beneath the television. "When your father left for Broadway or wherever he was going to make it as an actor, I always believed he'd come back. If not for me, at least for you."

Maxey was shocked. Her mother never talked about her father. She used to talk about him all the time when Maxey was little...not in school yet...when he would go away for awhile...come back...go away. Maxey was four when he left the last time. Whenever Maxey would ask about him, it would upset her mother so much Maxey would try to take back the words. She began to stutter. It was six years later, and now her mother was talking about him again. And she was upset.

Her mother said, "Your daddy's never coming back. He's gone for good."

Maxey bit her lip. Mama wasn't feeling well. Maybe there had been some misunderstanding. Maxey was convinced her daddy wanted to come home. She knew it took all his time to be an actor. Mama had told her so...a long time ago. *That's it! Mama is worried Daddy will be too busy to think about us anymore.*

"S..so, D..daddy is a famous actor n..now?"

Mama laughed—like the bullies laughed when they picked on Maxey. "He's living in Springfield, Missouri. They don't make movies there. If he's in the theatre business, he's probably selling popcorn. You see, Maxey, I've told you over and over daydreams and fantasies will get you nowhere. He wants a divorce. A divorce. Don't you see, Maxey? It's no good to hope for something that'll never happen."

Suddenly Mama sounded like she had the hiccups, but she didn't. She was crying. Maxey had never seen her mother cry like that. She didn't know what to do. She patted her mother on the shoulder, and Mama put her arm around Maxey's waist.

22

Maxey just stood there awhile, thinking about the letter.

Divorce? Some of Maxey's friends had told her about their parents' divorces. It meant one parent didn't live with you anymore. *Daddy doesn't live with us anyway.* Maxey's friends visited their moms or dads who didn't live with them. *Maybe I'll get to visit daddy now that he and Mama are getting a divorce.*

Maxey believed if her daddy really lived in Springfield, he must fly to LA or New York, places she'd seen on TV, and work as an actor there. As she stood beside her mother, she let her imagination take her far away...to New York City.

In her mind, Maxey and her father visited a restaurant where a man in a uniform opened the door. They sat at a table shaped like a horseshoe where they watched everyone eating dinner and everyone watched them. Her daddy asked her what she wanted for dinner. Maxey tried to imagine the menu.

"Maxey," Mama said sternly, "get your head out of the clouds and tell me what you want for supper."

Maxey shrugged.

"I don't feel like cooking. How about a peanut butter and jelly sandwich?"

Maxey nodded.

Mama flicked a crumb off Maxey's chin. "Eating moon pies again?"

"I..I only ate one."

Mama brushed her eyes with her hands and went into the kitchen.

Maxey tried to tell herself that her father wanted the divorce so she could visit him. She told herself, *I'll tell him I have the leading role in a play. He'll be so proud of me. He'll say I can star in a movie with him. He'll call me his little princess and put his hand on my head and smile...just like...he used to.*

Something wet and salty slithered over Maxey's lips. Stunned, she realized she was crying.

23

Suddenly her mother yelled, "Maxine!"

Uh-oh. When Maxey's mother called her "Maxine," it could only mean she was in trouble. Maxey wiped her eyes and answered, "Yes, ma'am, I..I'm coming."

Mama shook the box of moon pies at her. She said, "You told me you ate only one moon pie, but there are two missing."

Maxey hung her head. *How could I know she counted the moon pies?*

"Tell me what you did with the other one."

When the kids at school caught her drawing the man in the moon, they thought she was doodling "smiley faces." She didn't correct them.

"I..I..I made a face," she said.

Mama glared at her. "What kind of face?" she asked.

Maxey panicked. Mama hated lying worse than make-believe. "It was th..the man in th..the moon," Maxey admitted.

Mama threw the box of moon pies on the table and screamed, "Man in the moon! For heaven's sake, Maxey! When are you ever going to quit all this make-believe nonsense and behave like a normal human being? Show me where it is."

Maxey ran to her room with Mama close behind her. Maxey snatched the moon pie from the toy box and shoved it into her mother's hand. Mama squeezed the little moon pie in her hand. The eyes stuck together, and the mouth puckered in a kiss. Mama kept squishing it until the marshmallow filling oozed between her fingers and yellow crumbs fell to the floor.

The letter was making Mama do strange things. Maxey began to worry about the future—like Sunday night. She tugged at Mama's arm and asked, "Is Hallelujah N..Night s..still on?"

Mama stared at the gooey lump in her hand and then at Maxey. Slowly, she smiled. It was a tiny smile but Maxey liked it. Mama put her arm around Maxey's shoulders and hugged her tight. Maxey's face was squished against Mama's waist. Squished like the moon pie's. But that was okay.

☾

Chapter 3

The Vampire

*B*y the time Hallelujah Night was over, Maxey had emptied half of her sack full of candy. Little fingers tickled the inside of her stomach and the back of her throat. A gooey sweetness coated her tongue. Knowing how much Rory liked candy, she thought, *Too bad Rory didn't want to come.* She wondered what he'd meant by saying he had better things to do than play kid games or trick-or-treat.

She had never been trick-or-treating, but Hallelujah Night had to be better. She liked watching the grownups act silly, and the singing and Bible lesson at the end was fun. But she liked the games best. Everyone who played got a prize.

She fingered the prizes in her sack. Her favorite was a necklace of brown and white seashells. She had gotten it for catching the biggest bass at Go Fish.

If not for Mrs. Lopez, she would've had to give it back. Mama had been sitting behind the giant colored cardboard Lake Fork, safety-pinning paper fish onto the lines dangling over the top. When the number on Maxey's fish matched the loveliest thing on the prize table, Mama worried people would think she hadn't been fair. Mrs. Lopez, who dropped the lines over the top of the cardboard, had pointed out that Mama couldn't see who was getting the fish she pinned on Maxey's line.

Mrs. Lopez is nice.

So is Mama for sewing me such a pretty angel costume, Maxey thought as she examined her dress for the zillionth time. With her finger, she curled the silver lace on the end of its long sleeve. With her palm, she stroked the shiny slick fabric of the white gown. She glanced across the room where she had put the wings and halo for safekeeping. The sequins on the net wings twinkled on the floor like fallen stars. Her angel had won first place in the costume contest.

Angel would like me if she saw me in my lovely costume. Angel had bragged about going with her parents to some group's costume party at the Civic Center. Mama and Maxey weren't members or guests and couldn't attend. *But nobody would notice me,* Maxey reasoned. *They'd figure I was with an adult who belonged. I've got to find a way to get there and surprise Angel.*

Maxey knew the Civic Center was near the Dairy Queen. It never took long to get to the Dairy Queen to join friends for ice cream after Wednesday night church service. *It can't be far. I'll walk. It's dark, but I have my friend, the man in the moon, to light my way.*

Mama and Mrs. Lopez were cleaning the fellowship hall after everyone else had gone. Mama was on her knees, snatching crumpled paper fish off the floor. Maxey fetched her wings and halo and a small wastebasket from across the room. She set the wastebasket beside her mother.

Mama dropped the paper fish in the wastebasket and smiled up at her.

"Can I..I go t..to th..the D..Dairy Queen with my friend?" Maxey asked, holding out her wings and halo. "Here. I..I want t..to be an angel."

Mama hugged Maxey's waist. "You *are* an angel. Thanks for helping."

Maxey's ears grew warm. She knew she hadn't really been helping. She stood on one foot then another. *It's okay if Mama thinks I've been helping,* she said to herself, *if thinking so makes her let me go to the DQ.* She wished her ears would quit tingling. *It's not like a lie. Not really.*

Mama fastened Maxey's wings and halo. "You're going with a friend?"

Maxey nodded. Her ears burned. She knew Mama didn't mean imaginary friends. *The man in the moon IS my friend. It's TRUE,* Maxey told herself, swatting her ears.

Mama said, "Okay. If I finish before y'all are done at the DQ, I'll pick you up. Otherwise, just have your friend's mother drop you back by the church."

Before Mama could say anything else, Maxey ran outside. She shivered in the brisk night air. It was almost cold enough for a coat. The front parking lot was empty. She took a deep breath and began walking down Highway 37.

She passed the Lake Country Realty. A streetlight made its tiny parking lot glow like an orange coal. She scurried past a convenience store. As she tromped across parking lots and grass, she kept several yards' distance from the passing cars. Soon she came to a stretch of highway where there were no lighted parking lots or people. No lights shone from the buildings and houses.

CLANK. CLANK. She heard a noise behind her and froze in mid-step, slowly turning her head. SWOOSH. The Bicycle Boy—nobody ever said his real name—pedaled past without glancing her way. Maxey laughed with relief.

The Bicycle Boy was a young man who smiled and waved at everyone as he pedaled about town. Most people in Quitman smiled and waved back. Maxey especially liked him because he would race ahead of the ice cream truck in the summer, shouting, "Cream! Cream!" This gave her more time to run inside, get some money from Mama, and be back outside before the truck passed by.

On the move again, Maxey tiptoed into the yard of an old frame house. The front windows stared at her like two eyes hidden behind dark sunglasses. Her back felt like a lizard was running up and down it. *Like someone is watching me.*

She looked up at the moon. *It's just my old friend. He's watching me.* Smiling, she took a deep breath and strode across the yard toward a giant oak tree. As she passed the side of the house near the tree, she noticed how brightly its white paint shone in the moonlight.

Suddenly, she stopped. At the edge of the moonlight something moved. She squatted by the large bush near the tree and peeked through the leaves. She strained to divide light from shadow, to see lines and shapes instead of blurry blobs of dark.

Into the moonlight stepped a shape. It looked like a giant bat. *No...the wings are a cape.* She recalled seeing that shape on TV. *It's a...vampire!*

The vampire pulled something from the folds of his cape: a spray can. The vampire set the can on the ground below a side window of the house and began to pry open the screen. He removed it, tossed it on the ground, and slowly raised the window high above his head. He bent down to pick up the spray can and tossed it through the window. He put both hands on the windowsill and lifted himself up until his middle rested on the edge of it. Then he disappeared inside.

Maxey chewed her lower lip. *What's going on here?* The man in the moon hid behind a cloud. She shuddered. *I'm all alone—with a vampire!*

It was not the first time she had only shadows for friends. Whenever she felt alone or a little afraid, she used her imagination. She crouched beside the tree. Her body stiffened. She became Shadow. She imagined her black hair reflected no

28

light as her black lips curled in a silent snarl. She focused her keen black wolf eyes on the patch of moonlight a few feet away. Her pointed wolf ears twitched at the slightest sound of danger.

THUD. It was the sound of danger.

The vampire had dropped from the window onto the ground. He no longer held the spray can. Instead, he was carrying a bulging plastic bag. He tucked the bag under his cape and skulked toward the bushes.

Oh, no! He's coming straight at me! Deep in her throat a rumble grew. She sprang from her hiding place with her teeth bared, emitting a ferocious growl.

The vampire's mouth opened wide. His teeth poked out, sharp and hungry-looking. He lunged at her.

She opened her mouth to scream, but no sound would come. Quickly, she stepped back. Her angel wings caught the edge of the bush. Her foot struck something round. She stumbled and fell backwards, hitting her head.

The vampire stood over her. His ragged breathing cut the still night air like a pair of dull scissors. Suddenly, he spread his huge cape and disappeared into the dark.

The night was closing in over Maxey's head. Her eyes were open, but she could no longer see. *Am I turning into a vampire, too—doomed to live in the dark?* she wondered as she shut her eyes…and sank…into…unconsciousness.

Chapter 4

The Witness

When Maxey awoke, she heard the familiar voice of Mrs. Lopez saying, "Hello, is this the Dairy Queen? Do you have a woman there who is looking for her little girl? Yes, let me speak with her." After a pause, she continued, "Mary? This is Lucinda. Maxey is here with me. Yes, come on over."

Maxey rubbed her eyes and wondered, *What happened? Where am I?* She remembered falling…and a vampire! She sat up quickly. *Did he bite me?* She felt her neck. No blood. No pain there. *But, oh, my costume is dirty and torn and my head is throbbing.* Groaning, she dropped back onto the couch where someone—Mrs. Lopez, she guessed—had placed her. She remembered her wings and halo. *Probably all bent up.* And her sack. *Bet that vampire ate my candy and stole my prizes, too.*

When Maxey opened her eyes again, Mrs. Lopez was leaning over her. A brightly-patterned blanket covered the couch and wrapped around Maxey's lap. Mrs. Lopez pulled it up and tucked it around Maxey's shoulders. She shoved aside a large black Bible and perched on the coffee table beside Maxey.

"How are you feeling, Missy?"

For the umpteenth time, Maxey wondered why Mrs. Lopez called every little girl that.

Maxey mumbled, "I..I'm okay. Is th..this your house?"

Mrs. Lopez nodded.

Mr. and Mrs. Lopez were in charge of the Sunday evening house church meetings that Maxey and her mother attended, but they met somewhere else. Maxey had never been in the Lopez home before.

Maxey sat up again and looked around. Another colorful blanket hung on the wall across the room. The patterns were beautiful, but something wasn't right. Someone had sprayed orange paint all over the wall and the blanket, too. There was even orange paint on the brown and green carpet. Maxey wrinkled her nose. *It looks like puke! And that paint smell. Double puke!*

She asked, "What happened t..to your house?"

Mrs. Lopez patted her shoulder. "I'm hoping you can help us find that out."

The back of Maxey's head ached again. She groaned and lay back down.

Mrs. Lopez said, "When your mother gets here, Missy, she'll take you by the emergency room, have you checked out, make sure you're okay."

Maxey didn't want to go to the emergency room. *On TV, emergency room doctors run up to you while you're strapped to a bed with wheels and they poke at you and shine a light in your eyes.* Maxey knew people in TV emergency rooms were there because they had been shot or stabbed.

"Mrs. L..Lopez, he d..didn't shoot me or anything."

"Shh, Missy. Mr. Lopez will be here soon. You tell him what happened."

"Why d..does he want t..to kn..know?"

"Why Missy, my husband Mr. Lopez, he is a policeman."

32

Maxey crinkled her forehead. She'd seen Mr. Lopez almost every week in church for as long as she could remember. She never knew he was a policeman.

The front door opened, letting in cold air and Mr. Lopez, dressed in a policeman's uniform. He looked like a policeman in the uniform. Maxey didn't know why, but she was nervous seeing him in the uniform. She thought she might be in trouble for trespassing.

She said to him, "I..I'm s..sorry for walking th..through your yard."

Mr. Lopez grinned. His gray moustache twitched, and his dark brown eyes twinkled. He made Maxey's nervousness melt like chocolate in her palm.

Mr. Lopez sat in the green armchair opposite the couch where he could face Maxey. He said, "Maxey, you have nothing to worry about. Just tell us if you saw anything before you tripped and hit your head on that tree root."

Wide-eyed, Maxey said, "You d..didn't s..see th..the vampire?"

"Was he carrying anything, this vampire?"

Maxey pointed to a spray can, lying on the floor.

"Was he carrying anything else?"

"When he came out, he had a white bag l..like th..the plastic grocery bags at Brookshire's. I..I couldn't s..see what was inside."

Mr. Lopez asked Mrs. Lopez, "Is anything missing?"

Mrs. Lopez answered, "Some cheap jewelry and a few dollars are missing from the dresser. The new clock radio is gone, too, Victor."

Their faces drooped. It hurt Maxey to see them sad.

Mr. Lopez then asked Maxey, "Do you know how he got into the house?"

Maxey pointed at a window across the room. It was still open. Maxey thought, *No wonder I'm so cold.*

Mr. Lopez examined the window and then shut it. SLAM.

Mr. Lopez asked, "Maxey, can you describe the intruder—tall or short, slim or heavy, light or dark, male or female—anything at all that might help us identify this person?"

She nodded. "He was s..so t..tall he hid th..the man in th..the moon. Just l..look for a giant vampire th..that can t..turn into a bat."

Maxey studied their faces to see if they were happy to realize how easy it would be to identify the creature that had messed up their house and stolen their clock radio.

They weren't smiling.

Maxey felt like she had swallowed a pile of bricks.

Mrs. Lopez said to Maxey, "You lied to your mother, Missy, saying you were going to the DQ with friends. I know because I heard you say this."

Maxey wanted to explain, but one of the bricks was stuck in her throat.

Mrs. Lopez continued, "When you saw someone break into this house, you did a dangerous thing by staying. You should always run and tell an adult, not let some mean person see you and perhaps harm you. Right, Missy?"

Maxey bit her lip and nodded.

Someone knocked at the door. Mrs. Lopez opened it. Maxey shivered.

"Lucinda, is she all right?" Maxey heard her mother say.

"Mama!" Maxey cried out as she turned her head a little too quickly.

Mrs. Lopez whispered something to Mama, nodding sideways at Maxey.

Mama rushed across the room to Maxey's side. She said, "Maxey, you let your imagination run away with you again. You're hurt. And it could've been worse. When I think...." Mama began to cry.

The heavy feeling inside of Maxey grew as Mrs. Lopez put her arm around Mama and Mr. Lopez stared at his feet.

Mrs. Lopez sat in the brown recliner near the couch while Mama sat on the edge of the couch beside Maxey. Mama stroked Maxey's hair and asked, "Are you okay?"

Maxey nodded. She saw Mrs. Lopez shaking her head.

Mama said to Mrs. Lopez, "I'm taking her to the emergency room."

Maxey said, "Really, I..I'm okay."

Mama asked, "Maxey, can you stand?"

Maxey swung her feet off the couch. Mama helped her up. Maxey teetered but only for a second. Then she saw her halo and wings by the door. They were crumpled. The pile of bricks grew heavier and heavier inside her.

Her voice quivering, she said, "I..I'm s..sorry about th..the costume, Mama."

Mama put her arm around Maxey's shoulder and pulled her close. "The costume doesn't matter. You're what matters."

Mrs. Lopez said, "I found this behind the bushes." She handed Maxey her sack of candy and prizes. The sight of her seashell necklace, curled up in the sack, made Maxey feel a little better, like maybe one or two bricks lighter. Maxey clutched the sack against her chest, hoping it would make the rest of the bricks inside her vanish.

Mama took Maxey to the emergency room. The emergency room doctor didn't strap Maxey to a bed with wheels, but he shined a light in her eyes. As soon as he said that Maxey was okay, she and her mother went home.

Maxey wondered, *Why does Mama believe the doctor instead of me? What does he know about how I feel? I WAS okay, but not now. I'm so tired of carrying this weight around.*

Mama tucked her in bed, kissing her forehead.

Maxey closed her eyes. Her one last thought was, *I hope I don't dream.* ☪

35

Chapter 5

The Indian Princess

By the following afternoon, news of Maxey's encounter with the "vampire" had spread all over school like a flu epidemic. It seemed everyone she passed on the sidewalk murmured behind her back. Her classmates whispered behind their hands, pointing at her with their eyes. Bubba and Rusty pushed her into the dirt, raised their arms high like bats, and squealed, "We vant to dwink your blood!" At last, school was nearly over for the day—only one more class, the one Maxey now dreaded most: drama.

Before Mrs. Cannon arrived, Angel put her hands on her hips and glared at Maxey. She said, "Werewolf meets vampire—you could've sold tickets." She laughed at Maxey before turning to sit down. The others laughed at Maxey, too.

Mrs. Cannon stepped through the doorway.

Everyone got quiet.

Mrs. Cannon's gaze swept the room.

No one spoke.

Mrs. Cannon sat down at her desk and motioned Maxey

to come to her.

"Maxine," Mrs. Cannon said quietly, "I have to discipline you for not completing any of your reading assignments last week. You'll sit in the desk beside mine and write definitions." She handed Maxey theatrical terms to copy.

Maxey hung her head, grateful for the thin curtain her hair made around her face. She slid into the desk reserved for students who misbehaved and took out her pencil and paper. She wouldn't raise her head or even her eyes because she didn't want to face her classmates, her enemies—Angel being the worst of them. As she stared at the legs of her orange corduroy pants, she thought, *I can't let Angel get away with all her meanness. I've got to do...well, something.*

Mrs. Cannon was passing out stapled typewritten pages. When Maxey's copy dropped onto her desk, her heartbeat quickened as she stared at it. It was the Thanksgiving play.

Mrs. Cannon said, "Take these home. Decide what role you would like in the play. Read at least four lines of that role to an adult and bring a signed note saying you read the lines. Wednesday you can try out for the part."

Mrs. Cannon paused.

Maxey could feel Mrs. Cannon's gaze penetrating the top of her lowered head. It was as if her stare had fingers that lifted Maxey's chin until Maxey's gray-green eyes met Mrs. Cannon's brown ones in another long-distance hug.

Still holding Maxey's eyes with hers, Mrs. Cannon continued, "If you don't bring the signed note on Wednesday, you cannot try out for a part in the play. Instead, you will spend the next two weeks of this class in the library."

Maxey tore her eyes away from Mrs. Cannon's and stared at the play on her desk. The letters blurred. She wiped the corner of her eyes with the sleeve of her faded black pullover, determined not to cry. *I can't tell Mama I'm in a drama class. Spending time in the library isn't so bad.*

But she had already convinced herself that her daddy would come to see her in a play if only she had the leading role. Besides, being banished to the library would give the kids in her class one more reason to make fun of her. She knew she could pretend better than any of them. She wanted them to respect her. Starring in a play seemed just the way to make that happen. She hunched over her desk and gripped her pencil tightly. As she scrawled the definition of "tragedy," she thought, *No way I'm staying in the library. I'll get the leading role. I've got to.*

Mrs. Cannon began to discuss the various roles, saying this Thanksgiving play was unique in that the leading role was that of the Indian princess rather than one of the Pilgrims. Maxey's eyes widened and a smile dawned on her face. She could not have imagined a better role. She liked pretending to be an Indian more than anything else—except pretending to be Shadow, of course.

Angel announced, "I want to be the Indian princess."

Maxey chewed her lip. She made up her mind that nobody, not even Angel or Mama, was going to keep her from getting that part.

Chapter 6

The Homework

When the bell rang, signaling the end of the school day, Maxey marched across the schoolyard to her apartment and went straight to her bedroom, not even saying "Hi" to Mama who was busy in the kitchen. She shut the door behind her and threw herself face down on the bed. She tried to summon enough courage to tell her mother about the drama class, but all she could do was lie there, thinking about how much she wanted to get even with Angel.

Rory had been her only friend until she met Angel. Angel had moved to Quitman at the end of fifth grade. She and Maxey were in the same classroom. Since Angel didn't know anyone, she was eager to make friends. It was great having another girl to play with. Remembering the good times they had shared made it hard for Maxey to accept Angel's defection. Angel's cruel words and laughter felt worse than a yellow jacket's sting.

KNOCK-KNOCK. Maxey heard Mama's voice, muffled by the door, saying, "Get your homework done before supper, and we'll watch Monday Night Football together. It ought to be a good game: Green Bay and Dallas."

Maxey didn't answer.

She was still lying on her bed when her mother called her to supper.

Maxey pushed her food with her fork, eating none of it.

Mama said, "That's tuna noodle casserole, your favorite."

"I..I'm just n..not hungry, I..I guess."

"You're always hungry. What's wrong?"

"I..I n..need help with my homework."

"No problem. The game doesn't start until eight."

"Homework in d..d..d..drama class."

CLACK. Mama dropped her fork onto her plate. She stared at Maxey. "Did you say drama class? DRAMA class?"

Maxey lowered her head and nodded.

"What's this about you being in a drama class?"

"It's part of th..the fine arts elective."

Mama grabbed her fork and waved it in the air. "Of all the foolishness! What do those people at that school think they're doing, encouraging kids to pretend to be something they're not? Don't they know kids do enough of that already? At least you do—that's for sure. You don't need any class to teach you that." She shoveled an extra-large bite into her mouth.

Finally, she asked, "What sort of homework?"

"You've got t..to l..listen t..to me read."

"Read what?"

"L..l..lines in a play."

"A play!" Mama yelled. She pointed her fork at Maxey.

The way Mama was jabbing the air with her fork made Maxey remember the time she and Mama played with soap bubbles. Maxey blew them and Mama tried to pop them before they disappeared. Maxey knew Mama wasn't playing this time. The frown on Mama's face let Maxey know this wasn't a game.

Mama shouted, "That's great! First Max and now you."

Maxey poked at a piece of tuna on her plate.

Mama took another bite, chewed it thoughtfully, and then said, "Well, it can't do you too much harm. You already live in a world of your own. Besides, there's no way you'll get anything but a silent role."

Maxey shook her head. "Th..the Indian princess has l..lots of l..lines."

Mama set her fork down and leaned forward. She said calmly, "Maxey, you're forgetting something. You stutter."

Maxey bit her lip so hard it bled. Tears rushed down her face. She screamed, "I..I will be th..the Indian princess. You'll s..s..see! I..I will!"

Mama shoved her chair from the table and rushed to Maxey's side. She knelt on the floor, daubing Maxey's lip with a fresh napkin and drying her face.

"Oh, Maxey," she said softly, "I didn't mean to hurt your feelings. I just don't want to see you torment yourself by wanting something you can never have. It'll only bring you heartache. Believe me, I know." She pulled Maxey's head onto her shoulder. Holding her close, Mama whispered, "I'll listen to you read."

Maxey struggled to read four of the shortest lines spoken by the Indian princess in the play. Every word was like a soap bubble, floating out of reach. Her tongue was a fork, jabbing at the words, popping them before they could be heard plainly.

Maxey's head was drooping and her shoulders were sagging by the time the ordeal was over. Her mother wrote and signed the note for school before turning on the TV. Maxey took the play to her room and threw herself on the bed once more, this time staring at the ceiling.

CHINK. CHINK. Maxey heard the familiar sound of Rory tossing gravel at her bedroom window. He used to come over all the time to talk with her after his mother went out for the evening or whenever she worked the night shift at the convenience store. Maxey silently hoped, *Maybe Rory wants to be friends with me again. I could use a friend right now.* She opened the window and leaned out.

Rory stood a couple of inches below her, grinning. He said, "Saw your light come on. Got a question for you."

"Yeah?"

"You know that vampire you saw last night?"

Maxey frowned. "You th..think I..I made it up, d..don't you?"

"No, I don't," he said. "I believe you."

"You d..do?"

Rory smiled and said, "Sure. I just wanted to hear it from you. It was a real vampire. Not, you know, a person, you know. A real vampire. Right?"

"Th..that's right!"

Rory smiled even wider. He said, "Whudcha think? Was he scary?"

Maxey nodded.

"That vampire was pretty brave, going out alone at night like that."

"I..I went out alone in th..the n..night. N..Nobody called me brave."

"Yeah, well, you didn't break into a house and steal stuff. That takes guts. I say he's brave."

Maxey shook her head. "N..Not brave. Bad."

Rory smirked. He said, "I mighta known you'd think that way. You're just a stupid little girl."

"I..I am n..not!"

Rory laughed and waved good-bye to her as he sauntered across the yard between his bedroom window and hers.

Maxey watched as he pulled himself through the open window and scooted inside. She scowled as she shut her bedroom window. *Some friend you are, Rory Shaver.*

Chapter 7

The Leading Role

Wednesday was cloudy and cold. Maxey shivered in her lightweight purple windbreaker as she plodded to the drama class. A gust of wind raced down her neck, leaving its cold footprints all along her spine. *Even the weather hates me,* she thought, as she tugged at the heavy classroom door and trudged inside. Silently, she sat in her desk behind Angel.

When Mrs. Cannon asked for everyone's signed notes, Maxey was first to hold hers out to Mrs. Cannon's waiting hand. Maxey attempted to lock her teacher's eyes in a gripping gaze, communicating her need for the leading role. Mrs. Cannon barely nodded as she took the note.

Maxey pulled the play from her trapper-keeper notebook. She ran her fingers over it as if by touching the print she could make the words become a part of her. If Mrs. Cannon only knew how important it was, surely she would give her the leading role.

Mrs. Cannon began to call on students to read their chosen lines. Chris Ames read for the part of a Pilgrim farmer. Steve Byrd read for the part of the Indian chief. Elisabeth Diaz read for the part of a Pilgrim girl. Maxey knew her name would be called next. She took a deep breath and exhaled slowly.

Mrs. Cannon said, "All right, next is Maxine Dove."

Sitting up straight, Maxey read loudly…if not so clearly, "I..I am Running D..Deer. What are you Pilgrims d..doing here? I..I am princess of my n..native l..land. I..I'll give you Pilgrims a helping hand."

Ignoring the snickers of her classmates, Maxey's eyes probed her teacher's face for an expression of affirmation.

Mrs. Cannon smiled at her and said, "That was really very good, Maxine." She glanced at her grade book and called out, "Laremy Green, you're next."

Maxey focused all her attention on Mrs. Cannon, trying desperately to send her a telepathic plea. *Let me be the Indian princess*, she concentrated.

Several names later, Mrs. Cannon said, "Angel McGregor, it's your turn."

Maxey wished with all her might for Angel to lose her voice or be seized with a hacking cough. But when Angel finished reading her lines, the entire class (except Maxey) applauded. Even Mrs. Cannon applauded.

Maxey's heart hammered against her ribs as she searched Mrs. Cannon's face for an expression of hope. Mrs. Cannon was grinning so wide her face resembled a big brown "smiley." But the grin was aimed at Angel. Maxey's chest began to ache.

Mrs. Cannon said, "Let's see now…Masheena Moss, it's your turn to read."

After everyone had read their lines, Mrs. Cannon called out each role and the name of the student who would play that part. She finished by saying, "Angel McGregor will be the Indian princess." Glancing around the room, she said, "Those of you without lines can be extras or work on the stage crew."

Maxey's throat tightened. It became difficult for her to breathe. Her head throbbed. Sounds rushed together as if she'd been thrown into a swimming pool. Her sight blurred. A single thought crashed through her mind with the force of a tornado ripping through a pine forest: *I didn't get the leading role.*

She stared straight ahead, trying to remember the last time she saw her father. She had tugged on his pants leg as he stepped out the door. He patted her head, called her his little princess, and told her he'd be back. Then he loosened her grip on him, pushed her inside, and shut the door.

He said he'd be back, Maxey reminded herself. But her mother had said he was never coming back. *Never.*

The bell rang. Maxey remained in her desk, staring straight ahead.

Mrs. Cannon gently shook Maxey's shoulder.

Maxey blinked her eyes.

Mrs. Cannon asked, "Maxine, are you all right?"

Maxey couldn't answer. It was as if a giant rubber band throttled her neck.

Mrs. Cannon took Maxey's face in her two hands and turned it gently until Maxey's icy stare fell under the warm rays of her smile.

Maxey's lips quivered as she explained, "You d..don't understand. I..I've got t..to be th..the Indian princess."

Mrs. Cannon asked, "Why?"

Maxey pressed her lips together and clenched her fists.

Mrs. Cannon placed her big hands over Maxey's small fists, their tender embrace prodding Maxey's fingers apart.

As Maxey's hands opened, so did her mouth. Her words stampeded over her tongue like wild ponies, leaping over her teeth, pawing angrily at the air. She told Mrs. Cannon all about her father and her mother and about the divorce. She even admitted how that she had been counting on a star performance to get the other kids to accept her, even respect her.

Maxey stood, her hands still held in Mrs. Cannon's, as she pleaded, "Please l..let me be th..the Indian princess."

Mrs. Cannon was silent.

Maxey waited.

Finally, Mrs. Cannon said, "There is a part in the play, Maxine, a very important part. It's called the understudy. If an actress is unable to perform, her understudy performs instead. The understudy for the Indian princess would be her sister-attendant during the play and would have no lines to say. However, the understudy must learn every line of the Indian princess in case she is required to perform in her stead. In effect, the Indian princess and her understudy have co-leading roles."

Maxey's eyebrows raised. *Co-leading roles?* She whispered, "Can I..I be an understudy?"

Mrs. Cannon squeezed Maxey's hands before letting them go. She said, "Yes, Maxine. You may."

Maxey ran outside and saw Angel and Rose still waiting by the fence for their mothers to come pick them up. Maxey tugged at Angel's fluffy white coat.

Angel swatted Maxey's hand away, saying, "Stop that."

Maxey said, "I..I have s..something t..to t..tell you."

Angel rolled her eyes, and Rose giggled.

Maxey's hands curled into fists, but she crammed them in the pockets of her windbreaker. She said to Angel, "I..I'm your understudy. If you're s..sick, I..I'll be th..the Indian princess."

Angel glowered at Maxey. Then, to Rose, she said, "I guess I better not get sick, then, or Maxey will ruin the play."

Maxey's excitement shriveled instantly in the heat of her anger at Angel.

Angel ignored Maxey and continued her conversation with Rose, saying, "My piano recital is Saturday at three in the Civic Center. Come hear me play."

Maxey shuffled home, her mind buzzing with an idea as elusive as a honeybee in a field of wildflowers. At last, it settled on Angel's last words. *I'll be at that recital but not to hear Angel play*, Maxey told herself. *I'm going to get revenge.*

☪

Chapter 8

The Revenge

*B*y Saturday, Maxey had devised a plan to get even with Angel. Mama consented to leave Maxey at the recital and retrieve her when it was over, saying she'd use the time to shop for fabric to sew Maxey's Indian princess costume. Maxey spent all morning contemplating her revenge.

After lunch, she practiced for her own performance at Angel's recital. She cleared her throat and coughed. *Not loud enough.* She coughed again. *Better, but it's got to be LOUD.* With all her strength, she erupted in a violent series of throat-ripping coughs. To her surprise, the acrid taste of partially digested meatloaf sandwich stung her throat, making her feel nauseous.

Mama rushed into Maxey's room with a bottle of children's cold medicine, saying, "You're not going anywhere, young lady, with a cough like that!"

Maxey shook her head vigorously. "I..I'm okay."

Mama hesitated in the doorway. "If I hear any more of that coughing...." Mama shook her head then left the room.

Maxey brushed her forehead with the back of her hand. *Whew! I've got to be careful.* She turned her radio on, went inside her closet, and shut the door. There she practiced her coughing spell. She emerged several minutes later with confidence in her scheme and only a little soreness in her throat.

She pestered her mother to get her there early. Finding the right seat was everything. Scanning the aisles of folding chairs, she found the perfect position: two rows back, aligned with the piano bench, where she could be heard but not seen.

Maxey's feet dangled when she scooted back in the chair. Parents and grandparents trickled into the room. They wandered up and down aisles until settling in their seats. Normally, Maxey didn't like waiting. That afternoon, she was too excited to be bored. She kept imagining the look on Angel's face.

Reading the program she had received at the door, Maxey thought, *Good, Angel is nearly last. I won't have to wait long for Mama to get me after...after my terrible coughing fit.* The anticipation tickled Maxey's ears and ribs. She giggled.

The woman next to her frowned. The piano teacher was making a speech.

The first to perform was a small boy, obviously a beginner. He didn't act nervous. He was having fun. Maxey clapped when he finished his short piece. One and then another, the piano students played their compositions.

Maxey was surprised to be enjoying the recital. She was enjoying it so much that it stunned her a moment to see Angel, wearing a sparkling black dress and shiny black shoes, take her position on the piano bench. At the sight of Angel, Maxey's anger gripped her, and she gripped the arms of her chair. Timing was crucial. She was ready.

At the first note of Angel's music, Maxey doubled over in the throes of loud, hacking coughs. Angel hit a wrong note and stopped playing. When she started playing again, Maxey let loose with a noise that would have made a chainsaw proud.

51

Angel's fingers crashed into the keys with a hideous sound like a cranky blue jay. As she attempted to begin once more, Maxey erupted in more wheezes and sputters than an old motorboat. Angel stopped abruptly and hid her face in her hands.

Maxey swallowed the burning taste in her throat. She felt sick. Again, Angel started to play. Haltingly, she finished the piece of music.

Everyone in the room stood to applaud, but Angel didn't smile and bow. Instead, she ran off the stage, crying. Maxey squeezed between the grown-ups and hurried into the foyer where she drenched her throat at the water fountain. Then she hid in the restroom until the recital was over. When she came out, she heard what sounded like a kitten mewing in one of the side rooms off the foyer.

The door was ajar. Maxey peeked around it. She saw Angel, standing in the corner. She was making the mewing sounds, holding a tissue against her mouth to stifle her sobs. Her eyes were red and swollen. Maxey had never seen anyone so sad...except Mama the day she got the letter about the divorce.

The pile of bricks Maxey had carried inside her at the Lopez house was nothing compared to the elephant that stood on her chest as she heard Angel cry. Maxey slipped inside the room and shut the door softly behind her. She tiptoed over to Angel and patted her lightly on the shoulder.

Angel didn't push her away. Normally, this small gesture of acceptance from Angel would have lightened Maxey's heavy heart considerably. But Maxey knew that only one thing could ease the weight of guilt she felt: Angel's forgiveness.

Maxey saw a box of tissues on a table and fetched a fresh one for Angel.

Angel mumbled, "Thanks."

Maxey said, "I..I heard you play."

Angel replied, "Mess up, you mean."

Maxey said, "N..No, you couldn't help it. Anyway, you finished. Th..that t..took guts."

Angel sniffled. "Did you hear that racket—that horrible coughing?"

Maxey stared at her shoes. *Angel doesn't have to know.* She answered, "Yeah, it was t..terrible." Maxey's ears instantly became red hot.

Angel wiped her eyes and blew her nose.

Maxey said, "Everybody s..stood up t..to clap for you."

Angel said, "Maxey, you're really being nice to me. Thanks. I needed a friend just now. And after all the mean things I've said and done. You're okay."

Maxey hung her head. Only by apologizing for what she'd done could she hope to exchange her load of guilt for forgiveness. Until that happened, Maxey knew she and Angel could never be friends again. But Maxey had to ask herself, *What if Angel doesn't forgive me?* She knew the answer was the same either way.

She said, "Angel, I..I d..d..did it."

Angel sniffed again. "Did what?"

Maxey stared at the floor and mumbled, "I..I coughed and made you mess up. I..I d.did it t..to get even with you for being s..so mean. I..I'm s..sorry."

Maxey didn't look up, but she felt Angel rush at her like the heat that goes before a raging fire. With the weight of her whole body behind both hands, Angel pushed Maxey, making her stumble backward so hard she nearly fell down.

Angel screeched, "Get away from me!" She shoved Maxey into the door, screaming, "I hate you, Maxey Dove! I'll hate you for the rest of my life!"

Maxey hurried from the room, past the curious stares of strangers, into the parking lot where Mama was waiting to take her home.

She didn't feel like she had gotten "even" with Angel.

She knew she had lost…a friend. By confessing to her scheme, she had gotten rid of the elephant on her chest. But what remained was a cavernous hole in her heart, a great emptiness that echoed Angel's words.

Chapter 9

The Answer

Maxey didn't want to go to church with her mother. She was afraid people would see the hole in her heart and guess what she'd done. But she knew her mother would ask questions. So she went. She sat in the back corner of the partitioned space in the fellowship hall where sixth-grade girls met for Bible study. She hardly looked at Mrs. Lopez, their teacher.

After church, Maxey and her mother went to the Lopez home for Sunday dinner. Maxey's mouth watered as they all bowed their heads and Mr. Lopez said their thanks to God for the food. Since Maxey enjoyed eating quesadillas at the Ranchero Restaurant, she looked forward to trying Mrs. Lopez' Mexican food. She wasn't disappointed. The hand-made soft flour tortillas, fresh home-blended salsa, home-made chicken enchiladas and beef tamales—all were delicious. For dessert, they ate warm soapapillas with butter and raw Quitman honey. The hollow pillows of flaky pastry melted like sweet memories on Maxey's tongue.

After dinner, Mrs. Lopez asked Maxey, "How about

helping with the dishes, Missy?"

Mr. Lopez said to Maxey's mother, "Let's talk about costumes for the Christmas pageant. The church will provide all the materials. Just tell me what you need. We're so happy you volunteered to sew them."

Mr. Lopez and Mama took mugs and a thermos of coffee to the living room. Maxey followed Mrs. Lopez into the kitchen.

Mrs. Lopez washed. Maxey rinsed and dried. For minutes, the only sounds were: SQUEEGE-SQUEEGE, PLOP, DRIP-DRIP, MIFF-MIFF, CLINK.

Finally, Mrs. Lopez said, "Missy, you weren't yourself this morning."

"I..I wasn't pretending t..to be s..someone else. Honest!"

Mrs. Lopez laughed, her black eyes sparkling. "That's not what I meant."

She plucked another cheesy pan from the sudsy sink and began to scrub. SQUEEGE-SQUEEGE-SQUEEGE-SQUEEGE. "I mean, Missy, you don't seem very lively today. Your chin is down a lot here lately. What's the matter with you?"

Maxey hung her head and whispered, "You s..see th..the hole in me." Without realizing it, she let water drip from the plate in her hand onto the floor.

Mrs. Lopez took the plate from Maxey. "Just what made this hole in you?"

"I..I was mean t..to a friend yesterday."

"And you want to tell me about it?"

Maxey glanced over her shoulder toward the living room. Soft sounds of conversation reassured Maxey that Mama wouldn't hear what she had to say.

Maxey nodded.

Mrs. Lopez handed the dish back to Maxey.

Maxey wiped the dish with a towel. MIFF-MIFF. In brief sentences barely above a whisper, Maxey told Mrs. Lopez about Angel—about their friendship...and betrayal. Part of her expected Mrs. Lopez to yell at her. But another part expected Mrs. Lopez to point out a different way of looking at things.

Mrs. Lopez replied, "Sounds like you need to ask God to fill the emptiness in your heart with love—His love."

Maxey decided to put that thought away in her mind like a piece of bubble gum in her pocket, stashed away until she could chew it slowly and deliberately.

"I..I have th..this other problem, t..too."

Mrs. Lopez wiped her hands on Maxey's dish towel. She asked, "How would you like some hot chocolate?"

Maxey nodded.

Mrs. Lopez took a plastic jug of milk from the refrigerator. She opened cabinet doors and took down a box of chocolate powder and two mugs.

"D..do you have marshmallows?"

Mrs. Lopez pulled a bag of miniatures out of a plastic canister on the countertop. She poured the milk and heated it in the microwave until thin strands of smoke rose from the mugs. She stirred in the chocolate, sprinkled the colored mini-marshmallows on top, and set the mugs on the table.

Maxey imagined the gooey pastel crust was the surface of a distant planet. The swirls of steam lingering above it was evidence of active volcanoes. She felt like an astronomer, viewing intergalactic dangers from the safe distance of her telescope. But she knew she couldn't keep distant for long if she wanted to enjoy the reality of the hot chocolate. She lifted the mug to her lips and tipped it warily.

Mrs. Lopez sat beside her and asked, "What's this other problem?"

Maxey clutched her mug with both hands and said, "I..I s..s..stutter, but I..I want th..the l..leading role in a play."

Mrs. Lopez silently sipped her hot chocolate while gazing at Maxey so long it made Maxey squirm. Finally, she said, "Missy, recite last week's memory verse for me."

57

Maxey raised an eyebrow. Nevertheless, she set her mug on the table and said in a steady voice, "'For with God nothing shall be impossible'—Luke 1:37."

Mrs. Lopez smiled and sipped some chocolate.

Maxey's eyebrows met together to ponder the matter. Suddenly, her eyebrows lifted. She said the verse again, clearly and steadily, from memory.

"I..I d..didn't s..stutter!" she exclaimed.

Mrs. Lopez licked her upper lip and asked, "Why do you think that's so?"

Maxey considered this for a moment. Suddenly she knew. "If I..I memorize s..something, I..I can s..say it without s..stuttering!"

Mrs. Lopez stood and kissed Maxey on top of the head.

Maxey stood on her tiptoes, grabbed Mrs. Lopez by the neck, and hugged her fiercely.

Chapter 10

The Understudy

*D*uring the next two weeks, Maxey memorized all the lines of the Indian princess, reciting them perfectly. Each day of drama class, she hoped Angel would have laryngitis. But Angel was always there, saying her lines flawlessly.

The Wednesday before the play, as she started on her way home after school, Maxey was reciting aloud, "I am Running Deer. What are you Pilgrims doing here?"

Angel and Rose were waiting for their mothers to take them home. Angel stepped in front of Maxey with her hands on her hips and asked sarcastically, "Just what do you think you're doing, Maxey Dove?"

"Practicing my l..lines."

Angel yelled, "YOUR lines? Are you planning to make me sick and take my place in the play? I wouldn't put anything past you!" She ran behind Rose, pointed at Maxey, and screamed, "Don't let her come near me!"

Maxey's cheeks flushed. She ran down the sidewalk and across the playground, not stopping until she reached the narrow street between the schoolyard and the apartments. She paused when she saw Rory talking with two boys on bicycles. She had seen the boys a few times since school started. She always hesitated to go near them. The back of her neck tingled.

"Hey, Dummy!" one of them hollered at her. "Cat got your tongue?"

The other boy twisted his mouth in a vicious sneer and demanded, "What are you staring at? Are you trying to listen in on us?"

Maxey looked at Rory, waiting for him to say something in her defense. After all, he had been her neighbor and friend ever since she was four and he was six.

Rory shouted, "Go on, Maxey! This is none of your business!"

Maxey clenched her fists. If Rory wasn't going to stick up for her, she would have to answer them for herself. But if she stuttered, she would make herself a target for their derisive laughter. She needed to recite something. Into her mind popped a memory verse that seemed appropriate.

She shouted, "Be not overcome of evil, but overcome evil with good."

Rory's face turned pale.

The other boys glanced furtively at each other. Then they shook their heads at Rory, jumped on their bicycles, and rode away.

Rory called out to Maxey as she climbed the steps to her apartment, "Hey! What did you mean by that?"

She paused and replied, "It was just s..something I..I could s..say without s..stuttering."

Rory let out a sigh. "Well, keep away from my friends from now on and don't be a pest."

Maxey frowned.

He grinned at her and asked, "Yeah, hey, how did you do that—not stutter, I mean?"

"I..I d..don't s..stutter when I..I recite."

"No kidding!"

"N..No kidding!"

Rory laughed. "Wait till I tell those two you were just reciting something. You sure had them worried."

"How come were th..they worried?"

Rory waved his hand at her in dismissal. He said, "Never mind. See ya."

Maxey started to ask him if he wanted to see her in the play at the Quitman Junior-Senior High School auditorium on Friday night. Considering how rude he had been to her, she decided against it.

Friday's drama class was exciting. Mrs. Cannon handed out copies of the winter play. The Snow Queen was the leading role. Maxey promised herself she'd spend all next week, the Thanksgiving holidays, memorizing the lines.

Mrs. Cannon prompted the class in a full rehearsal of the evening's performance. As the bell rang, she said, "Be at the auditorium by six o'clock."

Maxey used her imagination to transform herself into the Indian princess. *I'm the understudy*, she reminded herself, *and you never can tell what might happen.*

Chapter 11

The Play

*T*hat night Maxey and Angel stood backstage, awaiting their cue. Maxey's Indian princess costume made her look like the star of the play instead of Angel. Angel refused to speak to Maxey or even to look at her. Maxey ignored Angel, too, as she peered around the heavy velvet curtain, intent on scanning the audience for a glimpse of her father.

Maxey had written a letter inviting him to attend the play. She copied the address from the divorce letter onto the envelope, took a stamp from Mama's purse after replacing it with correct change, and dropped the letter in the street corner mailbox. She said nothing to Mama about this.

The dark-haired man sitting in the center aisle could be her father. Near the front sat a slender man with a moustache. He might be her father. If he was there, he would run to her after the play, congratulate her, tell her how proud he was of her, hold her in his arms. Maxey blinked hard and focused her attention on Mrs. Cannon, standing in the wings—behind the curtain at the edge of the stage—as she signaled the play to begin.

Angel stepped forward to meet the Pilgrims who strode across the stage from the opposite side. Maxey walked closely behind Angel, slightly to one side away from the audience.

The Pilgrims stopped. Angel and Maxey stopped. The Pilgrims stared at Angel. Maxey stared at Angel. Angel stared at the audience. Everyone waited. Angel had the opening lines. She opened her mouth, but no words came out.

Maxey's heart thumped against her ribs. *This is my chance! I'm supposed to take Angel's place if she can't perform. I'll be the Indian princess! Mama will be so proud of me. Daddy will be so proud of me, and everybody....*

Maxey's rushing thoughts screeched to a halt. She noticed Angel's lips were trembling, and then her whole body was shaking. Her cheeks were hot pink and her eyes were wild and glistening. It was then that Maxey realized the awful truth. Angel was terrified. And she was embarrassed.

That's how I feel when everyone is waiting for me to speak, and all I can do is stutter, Maxey thought. She remembered what Mrs. Lopez had said about letting God's love fill the hole in her heart.

Maxey began to shake, too. She was struggling with two conflicting desires. She wanted to show everyone she could play a leading role—one with lines—and play it well. But she also wanted to be Angel's friend and to do what was right. She felt a familiar tug inside her chest. She knew God was urging her to do right even though it wasn't easy.

She sighed. *Okay*, she prayed. She leaned forward and whispered in Angel's ear, "I am Running Deer. What are you Pilgrims doing here?"

Angel croaked, "I am Running Deer. What are you Pilgrims doing here?"

Maxey whispered again, "I am princess of my native land. I'll give you Pilgrims a helping hand."

Angel, her voice stronger and more confident this time,

repeated the lines.

And that's how they got through the play. Maxey whispered every line when it was Angel's turn to speak, and Angel repeated it. The audience didn't seem to notice. Even Mrs. Cannon and the rest of the class didn't seem to notice. Only Angel and Maxey knew.

When the play was over, the class stood in a line across the stage and bowed as the audience applauded. Mrs. Cannon motioned for Angel to step forward and take her extra bows as star of the play. Without warning, Angel grabbed Maxey by the hand and pulled her out front with her. Standing beside Angel, Maxey looked out over the audience, an inky pool with faces floating here and there. Everyone applauded. Maxey bowed and bowed...and bowed again.

Backstage, Angel took Maxey by the arm and steered her into a dark corner behind the replica of Plymouth Rock, one of the props the high school theater students had made for the sixth-grade production.

"Oh, Maxey, I was scared to death! All those people staring at ME and I forgot my lines. It was SO EMBARRASSING! But you were great! You knew all the lines. But you didn't let on it was you. Everybody thinks I was the star. No way! You were the star, Maxey. And my best friend in the whole world!"

The girls hugged.

Maxey's whole body felt like it was made of feathers. She knew at that moment she could dance on the wind. Something held her down, though—the thought of her father.

She ran up and down the aisles in search of him until her mother finally convinced her it was time to go home. As they exited the school parking lot, Maxey pressed her nose against the car window. *Did he come and was he disappointed that I didn't have any lines to say? Or was he ever really here at all?*

Chapter 12

The Spies

Monday, the first day of the Thanksgiving holidays, yawned at Maxey like a lazy hound. She was glad when Mama suggested they go to the church to fetch patterns and material for the Christmas pageant costumes. Angel lived nearby and Mama agreed to take her home with them if her mother would pick her up later. Maxey also liked to watch the comings and goings across the street at C.O.M.E. (Mama said the letters stood for Christian Outreach Ministries, Etc.)

As soon as they arrived at the church, Maxey tiptoed down the grassy edge of the parking lot and squatted beside a row of hedges along the building. From there, she could look across the back street and observe the C.O.M.E. building. (Churches and individuals stocked the small building with food and clothes to give away.) Men, women, and children streamed in and out like worker ants, carrying boxes of food and plastic bags full of clothing.

But Maxey didn't see any needy folks as she watched from across the back street. She saw spies. In her mind, those people were carrying top secrets and hidden weapons to and from their base of operations. She imagined C.O.M.E. stood for Criminal Organization of Murder and Espionage. She was responsible for taking notes on their activities and reporting anything suspicious.

She took out her invisible notepad and scribbled in invisible ink: *2 women, 2 midgets disguised as children – 2 boxes, 2 bags.* When she looked up, she nearly dropped her invisible pen. A familiar orange pickup pulled up to the curb in front of C.O.M.E. Rory got out *on the driver's side*, she noted. She thought, *That's proof criminal activities are going on there.* Rory and his mother went inside.

Maxey waited and watched. Rory came out, followed by his mother. He put a box of food and a large black garbage bag full of clothes in the pickup bed and spread a tarp over them. His mother sat in the driver's seat of the pickup.

The man who headed the C.O.M.E. operation came out. But before he could shut the door, Rory ran to him and said something. The man gave Rory some instructions. Rory nodded and ran inside the building. The man glanced at his watch. He waved at Rory's mother. She looked the other way. The man looked at his watch again, shook his head, climbed into his car, and drove away.

Rory exited the building again, carrying four blue plastic Wal-Mart shopping bags. *Bulging with…with what?* Maxey pretended to write in her make-believe notepad, *Parts of an alien spacecraft - smuggled as food and clothing.* Rory put them under the tarp. Now that the man was gone, Rory's mother left the driver's seat vacant for her son. Rory drove the pickup away.

As Maxey stood up to leave, she noticed the Bicycle Boy pedaling up the back street toward C.O.M.E. She squatted by the bushes again. The Bicycle Boy left his bicycle leaning against the building and disappeared inside. Maxey wondered, *Did Rory leave the door unlocked?* She made an invisible note.

When the Bicycle Boy came out of the building, he was carrying four blue plastic Wal-Mart shopping bags, bulging with...*with illegal weapons parts*, Maxey imagined. He set the bags on the ground beside his bicycle. He went back to the door, locked it from the inside, and slammed it shut from the outside. Then, he hung the bags on his handlebars, and with a wobble or two, he pedaled away.

Mama was calling, "Maxey, let's go!"

Maxey tucked her make-believe notepad and pen into her make-believe briefcase and stood up. She skipped to the car. They got Angel and went home.

As Mama pulled the car into the parking lot of the Wilson Apartments, Maxey noticed Rory near the street, talking with two boys on bicycles. They were the same boys Maxey had encountered with Rory before. Maxey's mother went inside while Maxey and Angel sat on the porch, observing the boys.

Rory reached up under the tarp in the bed of his mother's pickup and pulled out the four bulging Wal-Mart bags. He gave each boy two bags. They hung the bags on their handlebars and rode away. Rory turned and noticed the girls watching him from Maxey's front porch. He scowled and ran inside.

Angel asked Maxey, "What was that all about?"

Maxey shrugged.

"Oh well," Angel said, "I want to tell you about my idea. When I got home Friday night, I kept thinking about how you rescued me." Angel leaned over and squeezed Maxey around the shoulders. She continued, "After Friday night, I don't want to be Snow Queen in the winter play. But you do—right?"

Maxey blinked hard and nodded, biting her trembling lip.

"There's just one thing I've got to know, Maxey."

"What's th..that?"

"You didn't stutter Friday night! How?" Angel tilted her head to one side.

"I..I memorized th..the l..lines. I..I d..don't s..stutter if I..I recite from memory."

Angel smiled. She announced, "That settles it. We'll tell Mrs. Cannon we're trying out for Snow Queen as a team!"

Maxey stammered, "T..t..team? Huh?"

Angel explained, "You'll be the Snow Queen, and I'll be your understudy."

Maxey stared at Angel as though she were seeing her fairy godmother.

Angel smiled and said, "We'll learn the lines together. I'll help you memorize enough lines this week to try out for the part when we get back to school. Oh, Maxey, you'll surprise everybody! You'll be the Snow Queen."

Maxey recalled how Mrs. Lopez always said that God works in mysterious ways. *I'll REALLY have the leading role this time*, she thought. She would write her father another letter. This time he would be there to see her. She knew he would. Plus, the whole class would be impressed. She'd show them she could do it. They wouldn't laugh at her. Not this time.

Angel put her hands on her hips. She asked, "Well, how about it?"

Maxey grinned and shouted, "Yeah! I..I will be S..Snow Queen!"

The girls rehearsed the lines of the winter play until Angel's mother came for her.

Maxey went inside and overheard Mama on the telephone, saying, "Yes, Mr. and Mrs. Lopez invited us to eat Thanksgiving dinner with them. I'm glad you'll be there, too, Barry. We'll see you Thursday. 'Bye."

Smiling, Maxey thought, *I wonder if Mrs. Lopez will feed us turkey or enchiladas*. Remembering that Thanksgiving is a time of being thankful, Maxey prayed, *Thank you, God, for making everything turn out great!*

Chapter 13

The Theft

At noon on Thanksgiving Day, the sky was drizzly. The sun was peeping out from under a blanket of dark clouds as if it had no intention of coming out for the day. Mama covered her gelatin fruit salad and placed a dishtowel over a pan piled high with her homemade yeast rolls. She quickly set these on the floor of their ten-year-old hatchback, behind the back seat. Maxey positioned a pitcher of sweet tea on the front floorboard where she could hold it upright with her feet.

As Maxey was getting into the car, she saw Rory, perched on his front porch with his head in his hands, staring blankly at the drab day. The orange pickup was gone. Rory's mother must have had to work.

Maxey said, "Can Rory come with us t..to eat Th..Thanksgiving d..dinner? Mrs. L..Lopez won't mind."

Mama glanced across the yard at Rory and sighed. "Poor kid," she said. "I know Lucinda won't mind, but tell Rory to call his mother for permission."

Maxey waved at Rory and shouted, "Wanna come eat

d..dinner with us?"

It was as if she had plugged his face into a light socket. Glowing with a grin, he yelled, "Sure!"

"Call your mother!"

He disappeared inside and almost as suddenly reappeared with a can of cranberry sauce in his hand.

As he climbed into the back seat, Maxey, who was holding the front seat forward for him, pointed to the can and asked, "What's th..that for?"

Rory scowled. "Mom said I had to bring it—for the dinner, you know."

Mama said, "I'm sure Mrs. Lopez can use some extra cranberry sauce."

"Buckle up!" Maxey ordered everyone.

CLICK. CLICK. Maxey stared at Rory until he grinned. CLICK.

Maxey turned around. Mama pulled out onto the street.

Rory took his finger and pecked Maxey on the shoulder. She turned in her seat.

He whispered, "Did your mother say 'Mrs. Lopez?'"

Maxey nodded. She smiled and said, "Mrs. L..Lopez is n..nice."

Rory shook his head and whispered, "Not if she's that substitute teacher who got me into trouble last month."

Maxey whispered, "Maybe you d..deserved it."

Rory scowled and stared out the window.

Maxey whispered, "I..I'm s..sorry. I..I was just joking."

Rory ignored her.

Maxey frowned at him and turned around again. There was no way she could figure out what was going on in his mind. He had been saying and doing odd things ever since...*ever since school started...and those two boys on the bicycles started hanging around.* Maxey pondered this, but it remained a riddle.

As soon as she said her hurried hellos to Mr. and Mrs.

Lopez and the other guests, Maxey found the food. It was a personal duty to Maxey to examine the repast and rate it for quality and quantity. This dinner rated all A's.

Besides what Mama brought, Mrs. Lopez and some other ladies from the church had cooked turkey, ham, cornbread dressing, giblet gravy, and a host of salads and vegetables, including sweet potatoes with marshmallows on top.

Maxey hurriedly found the dessert table. She liked to walk around and around it, imagining each yummy-looking thing in her mouth. Scattered all over the table were pies—apple, cherry, pumpkin, and pecan—along with a coconut cake, a chocolate cake, chocolate chip cookies, and a banana pudding.

It was an enormous feast, but Maxey counted six adults and four children present to eat it. Gratefully, she observed the competition wasn't too bad since the other two children were still in diapers.

Mr. Lopez said everyone's thanks to God for the food, and they all sat down around two tables in the living room. Maxey scrambled for the seat beside Mrs. Lopez. Rory sat at the other table opposite Mama. A young mother set the infant seat holding her baby in the chair across from Mrs. Lopez while she settled in opposite Maxey. Her young husband put their toddler's high chair beside him at the end of the table opposite Mr. Lopez. Mama waved a man into the chair beside her. Maxey had never seen him, but Mama seemed to know him well.

After dinner, Rory and Maxey helped the adults collect the paper napkins and plastic plates, cups, and cutlery. They dumped them in the kitchen trashcan. After folding up the tables, the adults reclined in the living room chairs and sofas while the toddler played in the middle of the floor. Rain kept Rory and Maxey indoors. They sat on the floor, too, building a castle of colored plastic blocks.

Maxey had one ear tuned in to what Rory was saying to her and another ear tuned in to the conversation floating in the air above her.

Rory said, "Put the red one here on top of the blue one."

Mrs. Lopez said, "Victor thinks it's the person who vandalized our home."

Maxey handed Rory the red block and picked up a yellow one.

Mrs. Lopez went on to say, "Monday—right before Thanksgiving—this prankster stole eight people's little Thanksgiving turkeys. First Halloween, then Thanksgiving. The *Wood County Democrat* called him the 'Holiday Hoodlum.'"

Rory said, "I need that yellow block. Give it here."

Mr. Lopez said, "It's pretty low when a person will steal from C.O.M.E."

Rory grabbed the yellow block from Maxey's hand.

Maxey said, "Maybe th..the t..turkeys were in th..the Wal-Mart bags."

The adults all fixed their eyes on her.

Rory dropped the yellow block and the castle toppled to the floor.

Mr. Lopez said, "What do you mean, Maxey?"

"I..I was watching th..the s..spies."

Mama explained to the other adults, "Maxey lives in a world of her own."

Maxey tried again. "I..I mean I..I was pretending t..to watch for s..spies. I..I s..saw th..the Bicycle Boy go inside after everyone left."

Mr. Lopez leaned forward in his chair. "Did you see how he got in?"

"I..I th..think Rory left th..the d.door unlocked."

All eyes focused on Rory.

Rory scowled at Maxey and then stared at the floor.

Mrs. Lopez asked, "Rory, you were there at C.O.M.E. on Monday?"

"So?" he asked in a voice as tight as a rubber band about

74

to snap.

Maxey said, "I..I s..saw you go back inside. You came out with...."

Rory interrupted Maxey by blurting out, "Oh, yeah, that's right. I went back inside to use, to use the, you know. Anyway, I guess I didn't slam the door hard enough to lock it." He looked up at Mr. Lopez and said, "Gee, I'm sorry."

Mr. Lopez gazed at Rory curiously. He said, "That's all right, son."

Maxey answered, "Th..the Bicycle Boy came after...." She had started to say 'after Rory drove away' but changed her mind. She didn't want to get Rory into trouble. Instead, she said, "..after Rory and his mother left." She felt her ears redden and covered them with her hands.

Mr. Lopez asked, "Did you see the Bicycle Boy leave C.O.M.E.?"

Maxey nodded.

"Was he carrying anything?"

"Four plastic Wal-Mart bags." She paused. She had almost blurted out 'bulging with secret weapons' but knew what Mama would say about that. Instead, she said, "I..I couldn't s..see what was inside."

Mr. Lopez remarked, "Four plastic bags could hold eight small turkeys."

"And I..I s..saw th..the Bicycle Boy on Halloween."

Mr. Lopez replied, "That was the night our house was vandalized. Hmm. I'll have a talk with him tomorrow. Maybe he recalls seeing something. As for the turkeys, if he took them, I'm certain he meant no harm."

Mrs. Lopez stood and asked, "More coffee or iced tea, anyone?"

While Mrs. Lopez and Mama went to the kitchen for refills, Rory slithered around the corner of the living room to hide out in the hallway. Maxey followed and sat down on the floor beside him.

Rory hissed, "Leave me alone."

Maxey whispered, "You t..took four Wal-Mart bags, t..too."

"So? It was food. I forgot to get it when I went out the first time."

"Why d..did you give th..the bags t..to th..those boys?"

He mumbled, "Maybe they needed food."

Maxey smiled. "Oh, you were helping th..them. Th..that's n..nice."

Mama and Mrs. Lopez had returned to the living room and were passing out refills. Rory glared around the corner and whispered, "I hate Mrs. Lopez."

"It's wrong t..to hate s..someone. Why d..do you hate her?"

"Some guys brought a radio to school. They kept turning up the volume. Then they handed it to me and told me to hide it. Mrs. Lopez caught me with it. She sent me to the office and gave the radio to the principal. Those guys were mad. They couldn't get it back without getting into trouble. I hate Mrs. Lopez."

"Th..this was l..last month?"

Rory answered, "Yeah."

Maxey was silent for a moment. Then she peered into Rory's eyes and said, "Th..the vampire s..stole a clock radio from Mr. and Mrs. L..Lopez."

Without blinking, Rory replied, "Maybe he put it in his coffin to help him wake up at night." He jabbed Maxey in the ribs and laughed.

Maxey laughed, too.

Chapter 14

The Police

Maxey didn't laugh Saturday when Mr. Lopez and another police officer parked their squad car in front of the Wilson Apartments. She watched from her front porch as they knocked on Rory's door. Ms. Shaver answered, keeping the screen door between her and the two officers while they talked.

Soon Maxey heard her holler at Rory to come to the door. Rory and his mother stayed behind the screen door, and the officers stayed on the porch. They spoke quite awhile. Maxey strained to listen but she couldn't hear what they said.

After the officers left, Maxey waited for Rory to come out. Any day the sun was out, Rory would be out, too. However, the entire day passed and Rory never came out. By dusk, Maxey desperately wanted to find out what happened, but she hesitated. Rory's mother was still at home and Maxey was afraid of her.

Rory's mother shaved her head and smoked cigars. Her gravelly voice often screamed words that Mama didn't approve of. Maxey mostly dreaded the woman's tattoo. At the base of

Ms. Shaver's throat loomed a black widow spider.

Maxey remembered part of a Bible verse: "I will fear no evil." She repeated it to herself a few times for courage: *I will fear no evil.* She ambled over to Rory's apartment and knocked, backing away from the door before it opened.

Suddenly Rory's mother was staring down at her. A tall woman anyway, in her boots and cowboy hat, she was taller than most men. Maxey stared at her in awe.

Her boots, hatband, and belt were lizard skin. Her belt buckle was silver, decorated with turquoise. Ornamental stitching bordered the pockets of her crisp blue jeans, the legs of which were tucked inside the boots. Black fringe and pearly buttons decorated her western shirt. Maxey had seen such outfits at Canton's gigantic flea market and knew they weren't cheap. Rory had told her that on the weekends his mother was off work, she frequented honky-tonks and country-western clubs.

That must be why she's all dressed up.

Maxey tried not to look at the black widow spider peeping out of the top of Ms. Shaver's shirt. In an effort to look at her face instead, Maxey backed up another step and almost fell off the porch.

Rory's mother snarled, a cigar wagging between her teeth. In a voice that sounded like a growl, she asked, "What are you staring at, kid?"

Without thinking, Maxey blurted out, "You're all d..dressed up!"

In a softer growl, Ms. Shaver asked, "You like my outfit?" Turning up her lips to reveal yellow-gray teeth, she smirked and said, "A friend bought it for me. A good friend, if you know what I mean." She cackled loudly.

Maxey wasn't sure what made her more uncomfortable: the woman's words, her insinuating tone, or her raucous laughter. Maybe it was all three. Maxey stood on one foot then another, trying not to bolt like a skittish colt separated from the security of its mother's side.

With a snarl, the woman asked, "What d'ya want, kid?"

"Can Rory come out t..to play?"

"Naw."

"Can I..I t..talk t..to him?"

"Naw."

Maxey was stumped. Silently she prayed for an idea how to reach Rory.

His mother said, "Rory's grounded and I got someplace to go. So beat it."

Maxey dug her fingernails into the palms of her hands for courage. She asked, "Can Rory come t..to church with me t..tomorrow?"

Rory's mother threw back her head and guffawed. She opened the screen door slightly and flicked some ashes off her cigar. "Did you say 'church'?"

Maxey nodded. She fought the urge to bite her fingernails.

Ms. Shaver drew long and hard on her cigar before saying, "Humph. I've been wondering how to get even with that boy for bringing the police here. Church. That's about the worst thing I could force him to endure. Sheer torture."

Maxey started to say something in defense of church but decided it might be better to keep quiet.

Rory's mother slapped her thigh and shouted, "I love it. Yeah, yeah. I'll tell Rory he's got to go to church with y'all. What time do you want him ready?"

Maxey was stunned Rory's mother believed church was torture, but she was even more stunned to think, *Rory's own mother WANTS to TORTURE him.*

"Come on, I ain't got all day. I got someplace to be. What time?"

"At a quarter t..to n..nine."

"He'll be ready by eight-thirty."

79

Maxey was saying, "Th..thank you, Ms. Shaver," when she noticed Rory's mother had already shut the door.

Maxey was glad Mama approved of taking Rory to church with them. After supper, Maxey and her mother watched some nature videos Mama had checked out of the Quitman Public Library. Later, Maxey went to her room to lie down and think. *Rory is in some kind of trouble. But what?*

CHINK. CHINK.

Maxey grinned. She leaped from bed and scampered to the window, raised it, and leaned over the edge.

Rory stood grinning below.

"What happened? What d..did you d..do?"

"Aw, nothing. I needed to get into the school to tear up a letter I wrote about some teacher before she found it on Monday. The police and everybody's upset just because I broke a window to get in. No big deal."

"It was t..too a big d..deal. Th..the police came. And your mother is mad at you. She s..says you're grounded."

Rory shrugged. "You know, I could really be mad at you for giving Mom the idea of making me go to church."

Maxey frowned and mumbled, "I..I'm s..sorry."

"Nah, don't be. I'm not mad. I'm glad I'm going with you. That way I'll get to see some of my friends. I know some of them go to your church."

Maxey's forehead crinkled. "Won't you s..see th..them at s..school?"

Rory shook his head. "I've been expelled until after the end of the year."

"You s..said it was n..no big d..deal!"

Rory shrugged again. "I gotta go. See ya."

"Be ready on t..time."

Rory was already walking away. He waved at her behind his back before hoisting himself onto his bedroom windowsill and scooting in over the ledge.

☾

Chapter 15

The Plan

Sunday morning, Maxey was disappointed in Rory. After Bible class, he wouldn't speak to her. He avoided her until time to go home and then completely ignored her on the way. She tried to ask him if he liked the Bible class, music, or sermon. He refused to respond. He scowled at Maxey so angrily, she assumed he must have hated church as much as his mother hoped he would. That thought wounded Maxey's heart. Maybe Rory's mother wanted to torture him, but Maxey hadn't wanted to torture her friend. *IF Rory is still my friend.*

Monday, back in drama class, Maxey wondered if Angel's friendship had outlived the holidays. *Angel, will you stick with our plan?* Maxey asked silently.

Mrs. Cannon stood in front of the class and said, "I hope you all had a lovely Thanksgiving holiday. Now, let's get to work on the winter play. Who's ready to try out for a part?"

Angel raised her hand.

Mrs. Cannon said, "All right, Angel, you can go first. Will you be trying out for Snow Queen?"

Angel said, "Yes."

Maxey's heart thumped against her chest. *Come on, Angel, tell her we're a team*, Maxey pleaded silently.

Angel went on to say, "Mrs. Cannon, can we talk?"

Mrs. Cannon pressed her lips together a moment. She then said, "The rest of you look over the play while I speak with Angel." She motioned for Angel to stand beside the teacher's desk where they could confer in private.

Maxey bit her fingernails.

A few minutes later, Angel returned to her desk. Mrs. Cannon stood before the class and announced, "Angel and Maxey will both be trying out for the part of Snow Queen. If one gets the part, the other will be her understudy. Naturally, any of you are welcome to try out for the part of Snow Queen."

Rose Ravenwood snickered. She said, "You can bet Maxey won't be Snow Queen. It'd take her forever just to say the first line."

Several of the students giggled.

Mrs. Cannon stifled the laughter with a swift glare. Then, smiling, she said, "I think we will all be surprised." Gazing at Maxey, she said, "I certainly hope so." She gave Maxey a visual hug and asked, "Are you ready, Maxey?"

Maxey stood beside her desk, head high, and gazed over the tops of her classmates' heads. With all her imagination, she became the Snow Queen—regal, courteous, magnanimous. The lines of the play welled up in her like a fountain, as though the words of the Snow Queen were her own. But unlike her own words, the words of the play were calm and still in her throat; they didn't tremble.

In a clear and steady voice, Maxey recited the lines she had memorized with Angel. "I am ruler of winter and friend of the Frost Fairies. My carriage is a cloud, my horse a bolt of lightning. I dwell in an ice castle. I am cold but not uncaring. I cover the cold ground in a blanket of white. I clothe the trees in white velvet and with ornaments of ice. I am the Snow Queen."

Mrs. Cannon beamed a smile so bright Maxey felt as if she were standing in the spotlight. Mrs. Cannon and Angel began to applaud. Soon the whole class was clapping. Some were whistling.

Angel turned and whispered, "Way to go, Maxey."

Maxey's skin tingled with pleasure from the overwhelming adulation. Her body felt as light as a bubble. As she lowered herself into her seat, she placed both hands on top of her desk to keep from floating in the air.

Mrs. Cannon said, "That was excellent, Maxey, excellent!" She winked at Angel and said, "When Angel told me you could say your lines without stuttering, I'm afraid I didn't much believe her. But you did it. How? Angel wouldn't tell."

Maxey grinned and replied, "I..I d..don't s..stutter when I..I s..say s..something I..I've memorized."

A boy in the back of the class snickered.

Maxey lifted her head and silenced him with a smile.

Mrs. Cannon said, "Angel must do well, too, since y'all are a team."

Angel recited the same lines. She did well, but it was obvious Maxey had clinched the part.

After class, Maxey and Angel skipped down the sidewalk together.

Angel laughed and said, "Maxey, you sure surprised everyone. You did."

Maxey laughed, too. She gave Angel a hug and said, "Th..thanks."

Angel replied, "Thank me by being the best Snow Queen ever. Don't let me down, Maxey. I'd never be your understudy if I thought you'd leave me to stand on stage and face all those people alone. No more stage fright for me!"

Maxey said, "D..don't worry."

Angel's mother drove up to the fence that separated the

sidewalk from the parking lot. Maxey waved as Angel rode away. Then, turning to go home, Maxey paused as she heard someone say Rory's name. Two boys in her drama class, Chris and Steve, were talking. Maxey eavesdropped.

"My brother says he stole some CD-ROMs from the high school PC lab."

"No kidding! Hey, somebody stole some turkeys from C.O.M.E., too."

"No kidding! Hey, what'd you have for Thanksgiving dinner?"

The boys didn't mention Rory again.

Maxey wandered home, turning this new information over in her mind like a wienie on a wire clothes hanger, dangling over a small bonfire. Rory's lie burned in her brain like a charred spot on that wienie. Maxey was puzzled most about one thing: *Why steal CD-ROMs? Rory doesn't have a PC.*

Just as Maxey climbed the steps to her apartment, rain fell. Maxey groaned. *No way I can ask Rory about it until this rain lets up.*

She went inside. Mama was sewing. Maxey stood quietly beside the sewing machine until Mama looked up.

Mama's lap was draped in red satin. Maxey guessed she was sewing one of the wise men's costumes for the church's Christmas pageant. Mama held one corner of the material firmly poised beneath the sewing machine needle.

Maxey asked, "Will you make me a S..Snow Queen costume?"

Mama partially relaxed her grip on the end of the satin. She said, "Good for you! You were such a good understudy for the lead last time, your teacher is letting you do it again, huh?"

Maxey shook her head. She said, "I..I'm th..the S..Snow Queen. Angel is my understudy."

Mama tightened her grip on the satin. "Does the Snow Queen have lines?"

Maxey nodded. "L..lots."

Mama let go of the red satin and it slithered onto the floor. Putting her arm around Maxey's waist, she said, "That's wonderful, Maxey, but how?"

Maxey replied, "Just l..listen t..to th..this." She backed up a step and stood up straight, viewing herself in the video of her mind: a royal person of great importance. Plainly and without hesitation, she recited some lines from the play.

When she finished, her mother squeezed her tightly around the waist.

Maxey was dismayed to see that Mama was crying. "You d..didn't l..like it?"

Mama wiped her eyes with the back of her hand and said, "It was beautiful, Maxey. It was the most beautiful thing I've ever heard."

Maxey beamed. "Gee, I..I d..didn't kn..know it was th..that good!"

Mama said, "You didn't stutter! That's what's so wonderful."

"Oh, th..that," Maxey stated matter-of-factly. "I..I n..never s..stutter when I..I recite."

"I'm so proud of you, Maxey."

Maxey grinned.

Mama said," I didn't think you could make your dreams come true, but you did. You know, I've been thinking of taking in sewing. There aren't any stores here that sell costumes, formal dresses, men's suits and such. Besides, I've always wanted to do something creative, maybe design clothes and start my own dress shop. I enjoy my job, but it's hard on my back. Maybe I can quit it someday and start a business of my own. You know, that's a big dream. I've been a little scared and worried I'd fail."

Mama began to twirl the end of her shoulder-length hair around her forefinger and said softly, "You made your dreams a reality, Maxey. Who knows? Maybe mine will come true, too."

86

Chapter 16

The Night Out

When Maxey came home from school on Friday, she knew something was wrong. The apartment was so clean the kitchen floor squeaked when she walked on it. Costume materials lay in neatly-folded piles around the sewing machine. Mama spent most of the afternoon in her room. An unaccustomed chill in the air kept Maxey indoors. She listened to music in her bedroom until Mama called her to supper.

Mama had made chili con carne from her own special recipe. It was mildly spicy. Maxey ate it with corn chips and cheese. She ate alone. Mama was preoccupied. Mama was dressing up.

Maxey watched silently through the open door of Mama's bedroom as Mama strode from the closet to the bathroom, back and forth, time and again. Mama wore a red, white, and blue plaid skirt with a loose red sweater and red high heels. And makeup. And her best perfume. Mama even got out her curling iron and did her hair. These observations settled in Maxey's stomach like liver and onions.

Maxey started to ask Mama what was going on, but she didn't. She was afraid she wouldn't like the answer. She hurriedly ate her chili, chips, and cheese. Then she fled to hide out in her room, locking the door before throwing herself onto the bed. Lying on her back, staring at the ceiling, she tried not to imagine what was about to happen.

The doorbell rang.

Maxey began to fixate on a chip in the paint on her bedroom ceiling.

Mama's voice was louder and merrier than usual. She said, "Hello, Barry. Come on in."

The door shut.

Maxey's skin itched as she felt an unwanted presence invading her home.

Mama knocked on Maxey's bedroom door and called, "Maxey, come out here a minute and say hello to Barry Hart, a friend of mine from Bible class."

Maxey said, "I..I'm n..not feeling well. N..next t..time, okay?"

Mama tried the doorknob and sighed. "Listen, we're going to Clear Lakes Restaurant. We'll be back in less than an hour. I'm locking the front door. Stay inside and don't answer the door or the phone. Hear me?"

"Uh..huh," Maxey mumbled.

Next, she heard sounds: Mama shutting and locking the front door, shoes thumping down the steps, a car engine, tires crunching gravel, and then silence.

Maxey got up and poked her head out the door of her room. The living room reeked with cologne—Mama's and the man's.

Maxey unlocked and opened the front door. A cold blast of air penetrated her body like a sword. She welcomed it, inhaling greedily. She felt the air inside the apartment was impossible to breathe, oppressively heavy with the stench of deceit. Angrily, she realized Mama and Rory had been hiding things from her.

She stood before the open door and began to kung fu fight the dark chill. With every punch, she envisioned a face—sometimes her mother's, sometimes Rory's, sometimes a man's face without features. Maxey kicked more fiercely at that face. It represented the stranger who had taken her mother away.

As she struggled against it, a secret surfaced in Maxey's thoughts: the man's featureless face represented her father, too. Wildly, she punched and kicked, beating the face and its secret thought down, down into the deep well of her soul. She drowned the secret in the cold water of her unwept tears.

The wind gave Maxey an excuse to shiver as she shook with rage. She could confront one traitor tonight: Rory. Cold or not, no matter what Mama had said about staying inside, Maxey ran out the door, forgetting to shut it completely.

The orange pickup was gone. Rory was alone.

Maxey beat on Rory's front door with her fist.

She saw Rory peek at her from the living room window before opening the door. He peered around the edge of the door, saying, "Huh?"

Maxey said, "Get out here and t..talk t..to me, Rory."

"It's cold out there."

"I..I can s..stand it. I..I'm just a l..little girl, remember?"

Rory scowled. "Lemme get my jacket," he said. In a minute, he came outside and sat with Maxey on the steps. "You sure you don't want to sit inside?"

Maxey shook her head.

Rory shrugged. He asked, "Well, what d'ya want?"

"Th..the truth."

Rory looked away. He muttered, "About what?"

"You broke into th..the high s..school PC l..lab, d..didn't you?"

Without facing her, he replied, "So what?"

89

"You l..lied t..to me."

"Okay, so I lied."

"You d..don't even have a PC."

"I did it for some friends."

"S..some friends!"

Rory stood up. He asked, "Is that all you want?"

"N..No." Maxey bit her lip and stifled the urge to scream her thoughts: *I want US to be friends again*! *No lies. No silent treatment. Just be nice to me.*

Out loud, she said, "I..I want t..to kn..know what you th..thought about church."

Rory replied, "What's it to you?"

"I..I n..never wanted t..to torture you."

Rory laughed. He sat down beside Maxey again and said, "Don't worry. I told you I liked being able to see my friends there. Besides, the music was great."

"You were s..sad—or angry."

"Yeah, well, that's 'cause my Bible teacher turned out to be Mr. Lopez."

"S..so?"

"So," Rory answered, "I hate Mr. and Mrs. Lopez."

"It's n..not good t..to hate people."

Rory glared at her and said, "I don't care. They make me sick, talking all the time about God and about right and wrong. Maybe I don't care what God or anybody else says about what's right or wrong. I do what I want to do. Got that?"

Maxey peered into Rory's face and said, "You d..do and you'll pay."

Rory looked away. He replied, "Says who?"

"God. In th..the Bible."

Rory pulled his jacket tighter around him. He asked, "Aren't you cold?"

Maxey shook her head.

"Come on, you're shivering."

90

Maxey shook her head.

"Well, I am. I'm going inside." Rory stood.

Maxey just sat there.

Rory paused, holding the screen door. "Hey, Maxey, what's eating you?"

Maxey didn't answer.

Rory muttered, "Okay then."

She heard Rory shut his front door and lock it.

Leaping to her feet, she ran into the night. She raced to the swing set behind the apartments where she had spent many happy moments pretending to be a bird or an astronaut. Legs out, legs in, she drifted up and down and up again. She tilted her head back to see the stars, but they were hidden by dark clouds. The only light was the pale moon and a distant street lamp. Maxey and her thoughts floated in darkness.

Suddenly a bright beam swept across the grass as a car turned into the parking lot in front of her.

Oh no, Mama's back.

Staying in the shadows, Maxey quietly crept to the corner of the building. Crouching behind a tall shrub, she watched as her mother pushed open the front door and stepped inside the apartment. The man waited on the porch.

Mama reappeared in the doorway, saying in a high-pitched shaky tone, "Barry, she's gone. The door was open, and she's gone. Maxey's gone."

The man put his hand on Mama's shoulder and said gently, "Maybe she's just hiding. You look inside, and I'll look outside."

Mama disappeared into the apartment as the man descended the steps.

Maxey flattened herself against the side of the building and froze.

The man walked by her. Suddenly he paused. Slowly, he turned and held out his hand to her.

91

Before Maxey could stop herself, she growled at him.

In a soothing voice, the man said, "It's all right, Maxey, I won't hurt you."

Maxey let herself become Shadow. She bared her teeth.

Respectfully, the man said, "Even wolves seek shelter from the cold."

The cold.... Yes, it's cold. I'm cold.

Before the man could react, Maxey ran around the building and up the porch steps into the apartment. She heard his footsteps following her. She dashed into her bedroom, slammed and locked the door. Into her closet she ran and shut the door. She crawled into the far corner and sat on top of her old tennis shoes, her long coat tickling the top of her head.

She heard Mama knock on her bedroom door.

Mama said, "Maxey, come out here right now."

Maxey felt as if her stomach had wrapped itself around her backbone. She didn't like to disobey, but her body and her voice were paralyzed with dismay.

Mama ordered, pleaded, and cajoled. Finally, she said, "I'll deal with you in the morning, Maxey."

Maxey heard her mother open the front door. She heard footsteps on the porch. Next, she heard her mother shut the front door and turn the dead bolt.

Maxey stayed in her closet awhile, thinking. She thought about her encounter with the man. *He could see Shadow. Grown-ups NEVER see Shadow.* The idea was unsettling. If he could see Shadow, there was no telling what else he could see in her, what else he could know about her.

The one comfort she could cling to on this night of confusion was the shining reality of her role as Snow Queen. She wanted to become Snow Queen and leave Maxey, her old self with all her problems and fears, in the closet. With care not to make a sound, she opened the closet door and crept stealthily to her bedroom door. She held her breath and listened. Silence.

She turned the lock, paused to listen again, then eased the door open just enough to peer around it.

The living room was dark and empty. No light shone under her mother's bedroom door. Quietly, Maxey unlocked the front door and slipped outside.

She went to the swings again and sat there in the darkness. Mentally, she recited, *I am cold but not uncaring.* Cold wind whipped her hair and made goose bumps on her arms. *That's okay. I'm the Snow Queen.* Rain began to fall. Maxey held out her arms to catch the droplets. *These are my frost fairies, dancing in the air.*

Much later, she told the man in the moon goodnight and went inside to bed.

Chapter 17

The Lost Time

*T*he next morning, Mama's voice penetrated Maxey's sleep. "It's late. You can't avoid me. We've got to have a talk about last night, young lady."

Maxey couldn't make herself open her eyes, much less reply. She hurt all over, and she didn't know when she'd been so tired in all her life.

Mama moaned and said, "Maxey, you're sick." She placed an icy hand against Maxey's burning forehead.

As if to confirm Mama's diagnosis, Maxey coughed.

Mama put a thermometer under Maxey's tongue. She gave her juice and tablets.

Before Maxey could drift off into sleep again, Mama said, "You went back outside, didn't you?" She pointed to the toy box. "Your clothes are wet. If you weren't so sick, you'd be in a heap of trouble." Mama stroked Maxey's forehead and said, "Right now I'd just like to know why."

Maxey used the last of her energy to say, "I..I'm th..the S..Snow Queen."

Mama stood up and said, "That all depends on how soon you get well." She tucked the covers around Maxey and said, "Now rest. I'll check on you later."

Maxey slept most of the day. She dreamed Angel was the Snow Queen.

The few times Maxey awoke, she was tormented by the thought, *If I don't get well, I can't be Snow Queen.* Repeatedly, she asked herself, *How did this happen?* Every time her answer was the same: *Me and my stupid imagination.*

The next morning Mama said, "Barry is taking Rory to church with him. I'm staying home with you." She stooped to kiss Maxey on the forehead. "If you need anything, use this." She set a cowbell on the table beside the bed. "Barry gave it to me so you could call me without having to holler." She stroked Maxey's hair. "He's real nice, Maxey." She kissed her again and left the room.

Maxey groaned. *Mama hates to miss church. This is all my fault.*

That afternoon, Mama set a poinsettia and get well card on the table beside Maxey's bed. "Barry said to tell you he's praying for you." She set a small basket of scented soaps and lotions beside them. "Rory sent you this."

Maxey gazed at the poinsettia, too weak to reach for the card. The basket was covered in plastic wrap with a red bow on top. A name tag protruded from its folds. Maxey strained to read it. Lying in bed, she could only see: TO LUCI.

My name's not Luci. Why did Rory write that?

Monday morning, Maxey didn't go to school. All during the night she had tossed and coughed. Mama gave her liquid medicine to help her rest soundly. Maxey slipped beneath her covers just as sleep slipped under her eyelids.

Tuesday, after Mama took away her lunch tray of half-eaten chicken alphabet soup and cherry gelatin, Maxey reached for the basket on the table by her bed. She pulled the name tag off the plastic and read: *TO LUCINDA LOPEZ FROM YOUR SECRET SISTER.*

Rory had taken the basket from the table in the church foyer where folks often placed gifts for one another. *What kind of friend gives you a stolen present?* She pressed the name tag onto the plastic again, grateful it stuck. *Maybe I don't want to be friends with Rory Shaver anymore.*

She reached for the get well card. It was signed: *A friend, Barry Hart.*

Maxey thought, *He just wants me to like him because he likes Mama.*

Wednesday, Maxey was sitting up. She begged to go to school.

Mama said no.

Maxey reminded herself, *I've got to memorize ALL the lines. I've got to show Mrs. Cannon I can do it.* Refusing the liquid medicine that made her sleepy, Maxey sat up in bed, studying the winter play. She concentrated so hard on the play, her head hurt again. By bedtime, she was coughing and her fever was up. Mama scolded her for not resting and insisted on giving her the liquid medicine.

Thursday Mama told Maxey she couldn't go back to school until Monday on account of her relapse. *I'm missing a WEEK of drama class.* Maxey's insides churned like the time she rode the tilt-a-whirl at the Old Settlers Reunion carnival.

That afternoon, Mrs. Lopez came by to see her.

"Th..this is yours." She gave Mrs. Lopez the basket of soaps and lotions.

Mrs. Lopez examined it. "Tell me, Missy, how did you get this?"

"D..Do I..I have t..to t..tell you?"

Mrs. Lopez shook her head. "No, Missy, I think I can guess." Then, smiling, she said, "We've been missing you at church. I hate to see you sick."

"I..I hate being s..sick." Maxey confessed how she had stayed out in the cold, imagining she was the Snow Queen, and had awakened sick, and how yesterday she had tried to learn her lines but made herself sicker. "My s..stupid imagination."

Mrs. Lopez said, "Not stupid, Missy, just out of control. Imagination is like a horse. It must be tamed to be of any good to you."

"I..I've just got t..to be S..Snow Queen. If I..I d..don't, Angel will hate me, and th..the other kids will make fun of me."

Mrs. Lopez replied, "Ask God's help. If He gives you the opportunity, take it and do your best. Whatever happens, trust Him, that He will work it out for good."

Maxey's lip began to tremble. "Will my d..daddy come t..to s..see me?"

"I don't know, Missy." Mrs. Lopez patted Maxey's hand, kissed her lightly on the cheek, and said good-bye.

After Mrs. Lopez left, Maxey prayed, *Dear God, please help me be Snow Queen and see daddy and tame my imagination.* She paused. Then she prayed, *I know You'll do whatever's best, but help me be good if I don't like it.*

Maxey decided to take her medicine and rest. When she was awake, she memorized her lines until she felt tired. Then she put the play aside and rested.

Friday afternoon, she heard a knock and glanced up to see Angel standing in her bedroom doorway, wearing the Snow Queen costume Mama had made.

Maxey's shoulders drooped.

Angel asked, "How do I look?"

Maxey murmured, "Great," and began plucking a thread on her bedspread.

Angel said, "I just came to bring your homework." She set some books and papers on the end of Maxey's bed.

Still plucking the thread on her bedspread, Maxey said, "Th..thanks."

Angel twirled around. She said, "Your costume is so beautiful. I just had to try it on since I'm not going to be the one wearing it in the play."

Maxey's eyebrows lifted. "You're n..not?"

"No! Mrs. Cannon is counting on me to be the Snow Queen since you've been out so long, but I don't want to be. Maxey, please, pleeeeez, get well."

Maxey said, "I..I will."

Angel said, "I'd stay and play, but my mother is waiting outside. 'Bye."

Maxey kept staring at the door, seeing Angel again in her mind. *Angel—in MY Snow Queen costume.* Maxey clenched her fist. Then she reminded herself, *But Angel says she doesn't want to be Snow Queen.* Maxey unclenched her fist and smoothed the pages of the play. *And I believe her.*

That evening, Barry Hart came for dinner. Maxey ate in her room. She could hear her mother laugh all the way from the kitchen. Maxey couldn't remember when she'd heard Mama so happy. Maybe this man was nice like Mama said.

Maxey remembered his voice, gentle and kind. *He gave the Shadow-me a way to get in out of the cold without making fun of me.* To her surprise, she began to imagine his face in the audience the night of the play. She imagined him clapping for her as she took her bows. The thought slipped over her from her head to her feet like her coziest cotton nightgown. She smiled.

When Mama came for the tray, Maxey said, " I..I want t..to th..thank Mr. Hart for th..the presents he gave me."

Mama smiled and brought Barry Hart into Maxey's room. He sat at the foot of her bed on one side while Mama sat on the other side.

"Th..thank you, Mr. Hart, for th..the flower and card."

"You're welcome. I'm glad you're feeling better. And call me Barry."

Maxey looked at Mama. Mama nodded.

Barry said, "So you've got the lead in a play next week. Congratulations."

Mama said, "Barry is directing the Christmas pageant at church, Maxey."

Barry said, "Say, if you'd like me to, I'll help you memorize your lines."

Maxey studied his face. His eyes and smile glowed as if a light burned somewhere inside him, like the Jesus candle Mama lit most evenings. *Can I trust him?* She made up her mind. Grinning, she said, "Okay."

"Good! I'll see you in the morning then." He and Mama stood up to leave.

Maxey's lips began to tremble, but she forced the words out of her mouth. "And Barry will you come s..see me in th..the play?"

With shining eyes and ever-widening smile, he said, "I'd be happy to."

Chapter 18

The Discovery

Saturday, Barry helped Maxey memorize her lines.

Sunday, Barry took Mama, Maxey, and Rory to church with him in his extended cab pickup.

Afterward, Barry treated them to the lunch buffet at Old Settlers Inn Restaurant. When Mama and Barry went back to the buffet for more vegetables, Rory asked Maxey, "What about that party they announced in church? Something about Christmas carols at the nursing home near where we live. Tonight—right?"

Maxey nodded. "After th..that, our Sunday n..night church group meets at a house. Th..There'll be Christmas presents and s..sweets!"

"Which is first—singing or opening presents?"

"We s..sing first."

"Are the gifts in the cars then—I mean, while you sing?"

Maxey nodded. "We park n..next d..door t..to Heritage."

Barry and Mama had returned and were seating themselves.

Rory murmured, "Yeah, okay, never mind."

When they got back to the apartments, as soon as Barry escorted Mama to the door, Rory asked Maxey, "What time?"

Maxey's face was as blank as a numberless wristwatch.

Rory explained, "The singing and the party."

"Oh, s..six. We s..sing. Th..Then we go t..to th..the party with presents and s..sweets. D..Do you want t..to come?"

Rory shrugged.

"Mr. and Mrs. L..Lopez always have extra gifts for guests."

Rory scowled. "Lopez, Lopez. How come are they always around?"

"They l..love people and d..do l..lots of s..stuff for folks."

Rory jabbed his fists in the air.

Maxey said, "Come on. It'll be fun. You'll s..see."

Rory jabbed his fist at Maxey's face, barely missing her nose. He laughed, sounding unpleasantly like his mother, and said, "I'll be there."

Rubbing her nose where the air from Rory's jab had tickled it, she said, "Be outside by s..six."

Rory sneered and snickered and ran inside.

At six, Mama and Maxey gave up on Rory. They didn't see him outside anywhere. The orange pickup sat in the parking lot. Maxey didn't want to confront Ms. Shaver. She and Mama had wrapped two inexpensive things they already had around the house to exchange as gifts. They put the gifts in the back seat of the car and drove the short distance to Burk's Furniture and Appliance.

Some cars were already there. They waited for the others. A few minutes later, they walked over to the Heritage Nursing Home as a group.

Maxey followed the adults, teenagers, and other older children up and down the halls as they sang "Hark the Herald Angels Sing," "Joy to the World," and "Silent Night." Maxey liked singing those songs, but her imagination was flashing images in her brain like warning signals at a railroad crossing. The sinews in her body were as taut as drawn bowstrings. Something wasn't right.

She argued with herself: *It's just your imagination.* Still, she couldn't suppress her agitation. The group passed the entrance, and she slipped outside.

From the sidewalk in front of the nursing home, she couldn't see the cars parked next door. She walked down the driveway. *Mama would say my imagination is running away with me. But I won't go near the street. It's okay.*

Her heart played a rhythm against her ribs like the beating of the drums at church. She pretended to be Shadow in order to silence her footsteps on the gravel driveway—after zipping her REAL coat for protection against the cold.

What?! Maxey stopped, aiming her gaze as straight as a laser beam ahead.

A security light illuminated the parking lot of Burk's Furniture and Appliance. Maxey tiptoed closer, careful not to let herself be seen.

Someone in a red stocking cap and shirt scurried between Mama's hatchback and Barry Hart's pickup, then stopped beside Mr. and Mrs. Lopez' white minivan—a long, flat, straight, shiny metal bar in his hand.

Santa! Maxey caught herself before she squeaked the name out loud.

Glancing to the left and right, the Santa slipped the metal between the front door window and weather stripping. Swiftly, he jerked up on it. The Santa yanked the front door open and began stuffing presents into a white pillowcase.

Maxey leaned forward. Her teeth were bared. Her lips were curled. She was about to crouch, ready to spring into the open. *No,* she told herself. *This is for real. I'm not Shadow now, and that's not Santa.* She backed up noiselessly until she was out of the Santa's sight and then ran to the nursing home.

She hurried down the corridor in the direction of the singing, ignoring the attendants who scolded her for running. Pulling on Mama's hand, she stammered loudly, "Th..thief! Th..the gifts!"

Mr. Lopez bounded down the hallway, much to the consternation of the attendants, while the rest of the group followed. By the time they reached the front door, Mr. Lopez was returning up the driveway.

Mama saw Mr. Lopez shaking his head and she asked, "Maxey, did you let your imagination run away with you again?"

"N..no ma'am."

As Mr. Lopez approached the group, he said, "Folks, all of the gifts are gone. Whoever took them apparently used a tool to lift the locks."

The group murmured and sighed.

Maxey lowered her head said, "I..I l..let him get away."

Mrs. Lopez said, "Missy, you did the right thing this time. Better for this Holiday Hoodlum to get away than for you to be hurt."

Mr. Lopez admitted, "I didn't get there fast enough to see who did it."

Maxey said, "I..I s..saw."

Mama said, "Not another vampire story, Maxey."

Barry said, "Mary, I think Maxey will give us a good description. Tell us what you saw, Maxey."

Maxey grinned at Barry. "S..someone d..dressed l..like S..Santa but t..too s..small."

Mr. Lopez asked, "What do you mean?"

"A l..long, baggy, red s..sweatshirt. A red s..stocking cap th..that was pulled d..down over his face. N..no red pants or black boots, just jeans and t..tennis shoes."

Mr. Lopez said, "Good, Maxey," and asked, "Anything else?"

"N..no beard. A s..small face l..like a boy's." Maxey put

her hand over her mouth. She crooked her finger, motioning Mr. Lopez to bend down. She whispered something in his ear.

Mr. Lopez straightened up and said, "I have a hunch where I might find the thief and the stolen gifts. Go on with the party and I'll meet you there later."

They did. An hour or so later, the group had devoured all the sweets (except the two fudge squares Mrs. Lopez stashed away for her husband). While they stood around the piano singing about the birth of Jesus, Mr. Lopez entered. Shuffling glumly in front of him was Rory. He was carrying a pillowcase, stuffed with small, colorfully wrapped packages. Mr. Lopez motioned for Rory to deposit the gifts on the empty table near the wall. Rory arranged the packages neatly around the pine and holly centerpiece.

Mr. Lopez announced, "Rory has something to say."

People stood or sat in silence, everyone's attention on Rory.

Rory looked up at the ceiling and declared, "I'm the Holiday Hoodlum."

Several gasps polka-dotted the room.

"I spray-painted the Lopez house and stole their clock radio." Rory rubbed the carpet with the toe of his tennis shoe. "I took the turkeys from C.O.M.E." He wadded the pillowcase in his hands. "I stole your Christmas presents, too." He hung his head. "I'm sorry."

Maxey said, "It was on account of th..those boys."

Mr. Lopez said, "That's right. Rory let so-called friends influence him to do wrong. Rory's already making some better choices though—like letting Lucinda and me sponsor him at the boys' camp for the holidays. He's also agreed to let me mentor him the rest of this school year."

Someone clapped. Soon everyone was clapping.

Rory ducked around the table and shriveled in the corner.

Maxey skirted the table and sidled up next to him.

"I..I th..thought you hated Mr. and Mrs. L..Lopez."

"Yeah, well, Mr. Lopez and I had a talk. I'll tell you about it sometime."

Maxey smiled.

Mr. Lopez leaned across the table and handed Rory a napkin. "Fudge," he said. "Lucinda saved two pieces for me. You can have one."

Rory grinned. "Thanks, Mr. Lopez. Thanks."

Chapter 19

The Spotlight

Monday, the north wind whipped Maxey's thin brown hair against her face as she walked to drama class. She was pulling strands of it out of her mouth when she noticed Rose Ravenwood waving wildly at her. Hesitantly, she waved back.

Rose tugged on the coat sleeve of a girl standing beside her. Maxey heard her say, "Maxey caught the Holiday Hoodlum. I have drama class with her."

Next she saw Bubba and Rusty rambling down the sidewalk toward her.

She mentally rehearsed two words she'd memorized for such an occasion.

The boys halted in the middle of the sidewalk.

Maxey lifted her head and said loudly and plainly, "Excuse me."

They looked at each other and then at her.

"Better move, Rusty. She's the one who caught the Holiday Hoodlum."

"Yeah, Bubba, we don't want no trouble."

To Maxey's astonishment, they stepped aside.

Maxey grinned. Being something of a celebrity appealed to her. All day, she had heard remarks about her role in the capture of the Holiday Hoodlum. *Now, if I can just keep my role as Snow Queen and do so well....*

Behind her, she heard Angel humming. She paused to let her catch up.

"Oh, Maxey, everybody's talking about how you solved the mystery of the Holiday Hoodlum." Angel gave her a squeeze on the arm and said, "Way to go."

They walked the rest of the way to class together.

Mrs. Cannon put her wide arm around Maxey's narrow shoulders and gave her a hearty hug. "Maxine, it's good to have you back."

When the class had hung up their coats and settled down at their desks, Mrs. Cannon made a few encouraging remarks about the progress of the play.

She then said, "After today, we have only Wednesday and Friday to brush up on our lines. Friday night we'll meet at the high school auditorium for a quick dress rehearsal and the final performance. Are you getting excited?"

Maxey and most of her classmates nodded enthusiastically.

Her dark chocolate eyes drenching Maxey in sweet encouragement, she asked, "Maxine, are you ready to rehearse?"

Maxey felt the stares of twenty-three pairs of eyes, including Mrs. Cannon's, tickle her skin as she stood to recite her lines. She cleared her throat and began, "I..I am ruler of winter and friend of th..the Frost Fairies." She stammered here and there as she said her lines and finally ended with, "I..I am th..the S..Snow Queen."

Maxey sat down and stared at the legs of her blue jeans. She could feel Mrs. Cannon's gaze warming the top of her head.

Mrs. Cannon said, "Be sure to keep working on your

lines, Maxine."

Without looking up, Maxey nodded.

Mrs. Cannon said, "Angel, come up to my desk for a moment, will you?"

Angel and Mrs. Cannon whispered as though sharing a secret. Maxey began to worry. *Angel wouldn't steal my part, would she?*

Angel returned to her desk without glancing at Maxey.

Maxey stared at the back of Angel's head, at her bonfire of hair. She remembered Angel in the Snow Queen costume. *What if Angel really does want the part of Snow Queen? What if she's been planning to take my place all along?*

Mrs. Cannon had Angel say the Snow Queen's lines, too.

Maxey admitted silently, *Angel's really good. Maybe she'd be a better Snow Queen than me. So what if I don't get the part?* Bubba, Rusty, Rose and the other kids had already quit picking on her. She hadn't even had to pretend to get them to respect her.

NO! I'VE GOT TO be the Snow Queen if I want Daddy to come see me. That thought flew from her mind to her heart, stabbing it like a burning arrow. Maxey wondered if her father would realize this play was on her birthday. *Will he be there this time?* She tried her best to remember her father's face, but she couldn't. She imagined being on the stage, looking out at the audience, but she couldn't imagine her father's face no matter how hard she concentrated.

The pain in her chest dulled to a tiny ache, though, as she remembered that Barry Hart would be in the real audience, sitting beside Mama.

After class, Maxey grabbed Angel by the arm and asked, "D..Do you want t..to be th..the S..Snow Queen?"

Angel shook her head so hard her long red curls whipped around her face. "No, Maxey. I don't ever want a zillion people all staring at me with my mouth hanging open and nothing coming out like that awful Thanksgiving play. I never would've said I'd be your understudy if I thought you'd let me down like this." Her face puckered like fabric being fed beneath Mama's sewing machine needle.

"D..don't worry. I..I won't l..let you d..down."

Angel's blue eyes were glossy with unshed tears. In a tremulous voice, she asked, "Promise?"

Maxey nodded.

Angel's lips stretched into a tiny smile.

Maxey said, "I..I've got t..to get home." She stuck her thumb in the air. "Got t..to work on my l..lines."

Maxey enlisted her mother's help, but it seemed to do no good. Every time Maxey opened her mouth her brain took a hike, leaving her tongue behind.

By Wednesday, it was difficult to tell who was most anxious about the role of the Snow Queen—Mrs. Cannon, Angel, or Maxey.

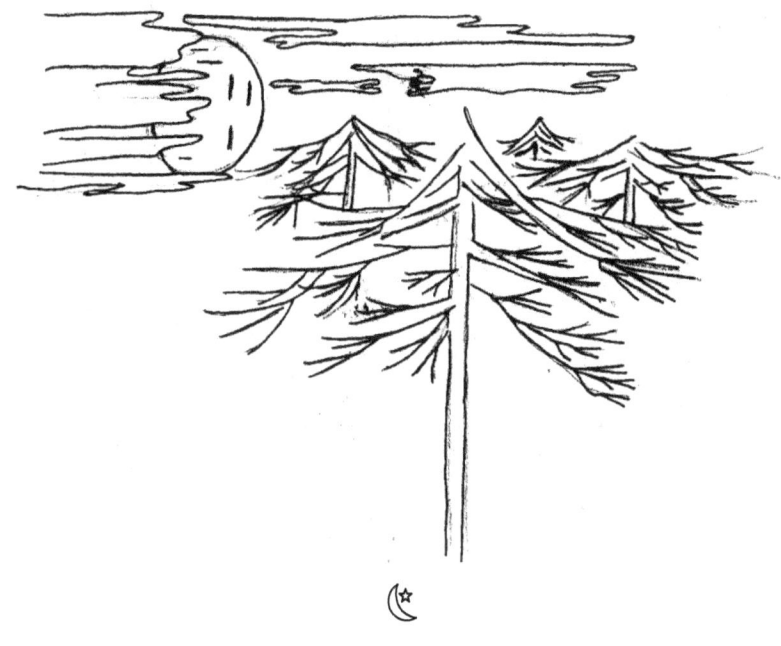

Chapter 20

The Snow Queen

Wednesday evening, Mama put her hand to her forehead. She said, "Maybe Barry will come over and help you before and after church tonight."

"D..do you th..think s..so?"

Mama telephoned. In less than an hour, he was there.

With Barry Hart coaching her, Maxey recited while setting the table for supper. She recited between bites while eating her supper. She recited in the car on the way to church after supper. And she recited after church until time for bed.

Friday's drama class raced headlong at Maxey like a big truck. She didn't duck it, though. When Mrs. Cannon called on her, she stood up straight beside her desk and mesmerized the class with her rendition of the Snow Queen.

Mrs. Cannon and Angel—especially Angel—beamed with relief.

A few hours later, Maxey and the others gathered at the auditorium for the dress rehearsal of the winter play. Afterward, Maxey stood gazing into the backstage mirror at herself wearing

the Snow Queen costume her mother had sewn. The dress was made of white satin and billowed with waves of sequined flounces, layered in loops like thick white frosting. The crown was made of cardboard covered in aluminum foil and costume jewelry. Mama had braided Maxey's thread-fine hair into a coil encircling her head like a second crown. Her scepter was a short twirling baton with white and silver streamers tied to the ends. Mama had bought a pair of white patent leather shoes and white lace stockings for Maxey to wear with her costume.

Reviewing the overall effect, Maxey said to herself, *I REALLY AM the Snow Queen!*

Angel came up behind her and said, "You look just like a Snow Queen."

Maxey smiled.

They left the backstage to get into position for their grand entrance.

As they peered around the heavy velvet curtains, Angel whispered to Maxey, "Aren't you nervous?"

Maxey shook her head, but then she admitted, "Maybe a l..little."

Before the auditorium lights went out, Maxey scanned the rows of faces. She saw no one remotely resembling what she thought her father might look like. Barry and Mama were sitting on the front row. Barry saw Maxey peeping from behind the curtain and gave her a little wave. She waved back.

Mrs. Cannon stage-whispered, "Frost Fairies in front, followed by the Snow Queen. Be ready to go onstage as soon as the music starts."

Angel whispered, "Frost Fairy—that's me. Well, Maxey, break a leg."

The music started. Angel and the other girls and boys wearing extra-long white T-shirts with white shorts underneath and knee-high white socks but no shoes trotted across the stage. They formed a semi-circle facing the audience.

115

Taking a deep breath, Maxey prayed, *Oh God, don't let me forget my lines.* She imagined her jitters were nothing more than cold ice cream hitting her teeth and tongue with a sweet chill. She swallowed them and stepped onto the stage.

Maxey turned to face the audience. The spotlight made a circle, and she was in the center of it. Everyone was staring at her, waiting for her to speak. A terrible thought occurred to her in that moment: *What if I stutter?*

She looked at her mother and Barry smiling up at her. She looked at Angel on the outskirts of the ring of Frost Fairies. She was smiling, too. Another thought came into Maxey's head and ate up the first thought like it was nothing but sour candy: *What if I DON'T stutter?* Maxey smiled.

Back straight, head held high, arms extended in sweeping gestures, Maxey raised her voice. In notes as clear as a cornet's, she recited, "I am ruler of winter and friend of the Frost Fairies. My carriage is a cloud, my horse a bolt of lightning. I dwell in an ice castle. I am cold but not uncaring. I cover the cold ground in a blanket of white. I clothe the trees in white velvet and with ornaments of ice. I am the Snow Queen."

Chapter 21

The Birthday

When the time came for the cast to take their bows, a wave of applause swelled from the audience, sweeping Maxey up on its crest and carrying her aloft in glory like an athlete propelled on her team's shoulders. Mrs. Cannon motioned for her to take her bows as the star of the performance. Maxey stepped forward.

Mama and Barry stood, then Mr. and Mrs. Lopez with Rory stood, and then other people stood. All across the auditorium, people were on their feet, clapping.

They're clapping for ME, Maxey realized. She bowed and bowed.

After the play, Maxey was thronged with admirers, congratulating her. Though she strained, standing on tip-toe, to see over and through the crowd, no man came up to her and called her his little princess and told her "Happy Birthday."

All too soon, it was over. The stage was dark. It was time to go home.

The front parking lot of the Wilson Apartments was

empty. Maxey trudged up the sidewalk and steps. She was lost in reverie, reliving the evening.

As soon as Mama turned on the living room lights, though, Maxey was yanked back to reality. Paper horns blew. People shouted, "Surprise!"

Maxey saw Mr. and Mrs. Lopez, Rory, Angel, and Barry Hart. They were grinning at her, all trying to wish her a happy birthday at the same time.

Mama had gone to the kitchen. She returned with an enormous cake in her hands. On it, eleven colored candles brightly burned. As if on cue, everyone sang "Happy Birthday" to Maxey. Careful to keep her costume away from the flames, Maxey inhaled, made a wish, and BLEW. Not a flame was left flickering.

Rory said, "Mr. Hart had us all park around back. Were you surprised?"

Maxey nodded vigorously.

Mama cut the cake and gave everyone a piece with some ice cream.

As Maxey was eating hers, Angel whispered, "What did you wish for?"

"I..I can't t..tell or it might n..not come t..true. I..I'll t..tell you when it d..does."

Barry stepped forward, a gift-wrapped package in his hands. He said, "This is from your mother and me."

Maxey thanked them and took the gift. She sat on the stool in front of Mama's easy chair and opened the box. Beneath a layer of packing foam, she found a pair of binoculars. They were small but heavy. A leather strap hung from them, and Maxey slipped it over her head so that the binoculars banged against her chest. Black and scientific-looking, they were a contrast to her Snow Queen costume. She raised the binoculars to her eyes. Everything looked fuzzy.

Barry asked, "Would you like to go outside and let me

show you how to use them? You can see the moon up close."

She nodded, thinking, *I've never seen the man in the moon up close.*

As they stood in the yard between the apartments, Maxey held the binoculars in her hands, hesitating, as she considered what she was about to do.

Barry asked, "Is something the matter?"

"When I..I s..see him th..through th..these, will I..I s..still believe in him?"

Barry squatted beside her. "You mean the man in the moon?"

Maxey nodded. "Th..the man in th..the moon is my friend."

"Are your friends always just how you like to imagine they'd be?"

Maxey shook her head.

"Are they still your friends?"

Maxey nodded. Carefully, she lifted the binoculars. Barry adjusted them for her.

Framed by the lenses, the moon was a bright orb, pocked with craters. Studying the lunar surface, Maxey was fascinated by its odd shapes and shadows. Lowering the binoculars, she stared at them, feeling their weight in her hands.

Before going back inside, Maxey glanced up at the moon, hovering over the pine trees. The familiar face returned her gaze, and she was sure her friend managed to wink at her with one of his craters. She smiled and winked back.

THE END